Edmund Gosse, Björnstjerne Bjrnson

Synnövé Solbakken

Edmund Gosse, Björnstjerne Bjrnson

Synnövé Solbakken

ISBN/EAN: 9783337385774

Printed in Europe, USA, Canada, Australia, Japan

Cover: Foto ©Andreas Hilbeck / pixelio.de

More available books at **www.hansebooks.com**

SYNNÖVE SOLBAKKEN

BY

BJÖRNSTJERNE BJÖRNSON

Given in English

By JULIE SUTTER

A NEW EDITION WITH
AN ESSAY ON THE WRITINGS OF BJÖRNSON
BY EDMUND GOSSE

LONDON
WILLIAM HEINEMANN
1895

A STUDY OF THE WRITINGS OF
BJÖRNSTJERNE BJÖRNSON

On a photograph of himself which Björnson lately sent to an English friend—a remarkably pacific person—he wrote in his bold and flowing hand, *fra hans Kjœmpefœlle*, " from his fellow-warrior." These words give an exact superficial impression of the temperament of the most breezy and turbulent, the most agitated and agitating of modern European men of letters. Georg Brandes has aptly said that whenever Björnson speaks, the flag of Norway seems to be unfurled. Yet a false idea would be formed, if it were not at once added that the primary attraction of this flag to Björnson is not the idea that its enemies are to be destroyed, but that its friends are to be gathered around it and to be marched somewhere. The direction and object of the march are secondary in the poet's mind. The great thing is to be moving on, with songs and shoutings and cries of defiance, tramping along the mountain-tops of the world, in the eye of the sun, keeping a sharp look-out for adventures and for moral princesses held in durance vile. This magnificent combative optimism of Björnson's is what distinguishes him from all his contemporaries. It makes his personality very attractive, and adds to it a touch of naïveté, of the happy, strutting child agog for pirates, which is quite unusual in our sated age. Norway supplies the oldest and the youngest-hearted of the authors of our time, the weary Ibsen huddled above the sinking embers of existence, and the schoolboy Björnson, climbing trees for mares'-nests, and flinging up his bonnet in the sunshine.

With these characteristics, and with a temper which is to a strange degree dogged and yet ductile at the same time, Björnson has been curiously modified by the tendencies of the age. By the date of his appearance, he belongs to the generation, not merely of Ibsen, but of Tolstoi and Swinburne, of Dumas *fils* and Zola, of Dostoieffsky and Renan. He has had to find his place among these extraordinarily diverse and unrelated types. At one or another point he touches each of them in a kind of unconscious or unacknowledged rivalry. In a certain sense, he has, in his restless questing way, tried the mode of each, and has been original in so many different forms that impatient criticism has once and again denied originality to him altogether. Now, however, that the body of his work is mature, and that he himself has passed into the sixties, we can more plainly than before observe a general tendency running through the web and woof of his multifarious writings, and we acknowledge in Björnson, no less than in the more solid and self-sufficing authors we have named, a consistent manner, a persistent intention, which lend to his work the character of wholeness which it once seemed to lack.

Every critic has noticed the curious division of Björnson's literary career into two distinct parts. The writings of his youth are separated from those of his mature age by a chasm both of time and style. For ten years, we may roughly say from 1864 to 1874—when at the height of his popularity and of his physical vigour—he ceased to write altogether, or else confined himselı to trifling repetitions of earlier successes. At the end of this period, he burst forth again with the old enthusiasm, the old volubility, but in a manner so radically different as to present the appearance of a totally new authorship. It is therefore impossible to consider Björnson's writings in their entirety without focusing the

critical vision twice ; the same glasses will not
serve to examine simultaneously his first and
his second manner. An attempt will be made
in the following pages to give some estimate of
each, and also to trace as clearly as possible the
inherent qualities which run through both and
belong to the essential Björnson.

Many of his apparent inconsistencies are explained when we recognise in the author of *Sigurd
Slembe* and of *In God's Way* the Janus-glance
that looks directly backwards and directly forwards at the same moment. Björnson is a
passionate admirer of the ancient glories of his
country, and has taken the viking and the skald
for his models ; in this direction, he is all for
individual heroism, for the antique virtues, for
the local and historical prestige of Norway.
On this side of his character, he is an aristocrat.
But there is another side on which he throws
himself with no less animation into the problems
of the future, is ready to try all spirits, to risk
all political and social experiments, to accept
with cheerfulness every form of revolution. Here
he is no less definitely and obtrusively a demo-
crat. The danger that waylays criticism in
endeavouring to do justice to the qualities of this
stimulating writer is that of confounding the
action of this double strain with mere feebleness

of purpose. The two ideals are really less incompatible than they at first appear. Their existence should at least offer no insuperable difficulty to those who are brought face to face with that much more bewildering inconsistency—the combination of mediævalism and socialism in the mind of Mr. William Morris.

I

The childhood of no other living leader of letters had been spent among natural scenery so likely to mould the imagination as that in which Björnson was brought up. He was born on the 8th of December 1832 in a solitary farmhouse, called Björgen, high up in the mountains, in the parish of Kvikne, where his father was priest. Kvikne lies at the head of the great valley called Österdalen, and on the very ridge of the watershed between the northern and the southern river-systems of Norway. It is, to this day, one of the most inaccessible spots in the country, and sixty years ago was a parish so much dreaded, that its cure long stood vacant. In the earliest of all his published writings, in the sketch called *Blakken* ("The Dun Horse"), Björnstjerne Björnson has given a vivid picture of the life up in the desolate parsonage, where

winter brought the darkness and the snow
sooner and kept them longer than in any other
part of Norway. The fierce landscape was
reflected in the savagery of the parishioners.
A predecessor of Pastor Björnson's had always
gone to his church armed with pistols; another
returned from his first service to find his garden
laid waste and his wife almost frightened into
fits by raiding neighbours. The latest incum-
bent had fled for his life, and had definitely
refused to return to Kvikne. The father of the
poet, after Kvikne had long been abandoned to
heathendom, had been appointed to be its pastor
because of his reputation " for steering a boat in
a storm." Here then, in the grimmest isolation,
amid the harshest and sourest features of natural
landscape, in an atmosphere of violence and bar-
barism, the first six years of the poet's life were
spent.

The change was abrupt, when the pastor was
transferred to Næsset, in the Romsdal, a spot as
enchanting and as genial as Kvikne is the reverse.
Many tourists pass this church every year; at
the top of the Molde Fjord the sea narrows to a
romantic estuary, the Lang Fjord, and far up this
arm of landlocked salt water, Næsset stands, on
the northern side, commanding the landscape
from its promontory; the village close to the

church being Tjelde. The impression of physical beauty made upon the child's mind during his brief stay at Næsset—for three years later he went away to school at Molde—has been recorded by himself in a very curious passage :—

"Here in the parsonage of Næsset—one of the loveliest places in Norway, where the land lies broadly spreading where two fjords meet, with the green braeside above it, with water-falls and farm-houses on the opposite shore, with billowy meadows and cattle away towards the foot of the valley, and far overhead, along the line of the fjord, mountains shooting promontory after promontory out into the lake, a big farm-house at the extremity of each—here in the parsonage of Næsset, where I would stand at the close of the day and gaze at the sunlight playing over mountain and fjord, until I wept, as though I had done something wrong—and where I, descending on my snow-shoes into some valley, would pause as though bewitched by a loveliness, by a longing, which I had not the power to explain, but which was so great that above the highest ecstasy of joy I would feel the deepest apprehension and distress—here in the parsonage of Næsset were awakened my earliest sensations."

Thus, in 1868, interestingly, but not in his best manner, in sentences which seem broken and troubled by some return of that overmastering vague emotion, Björnson describes the second home of his childhood, and the picture constantly recurs in the long succession of his works in prose and verse.

II

Björnson has explained that his early literary ambitions were divided between observing the peasant in the light of the saga and creating the saga in the light of the peasant. We may take the former of these first, although the two strains ran side by side throughout the labours of some twenty years. The earliest published story oɪ Björnson which we possess is, I believe, a little sketch called *Thrond*, which has unduly escaped the notice of the critics. It dates from the year 1856, when Björnson, a lad of four and twenty, was making a scanty living by journalism in Christiania. It has this peculiarity, that we find in it, so far as the outer form is concerned, no immaturity or crudity. *Thrond* is composed, with absolute firmness of touch, in the style invented by Björnson for his pastoral stories, and it is no better and no worse, in this respect, than the more ambitious novels which succeeded it. It might be taken as a model in miniature of the class of *bonde-novellen*.

To realise how original such a piece of writing as *Thrond* must have seemed to attentive readers, we need to know how unparalleled it was in Scandinavian literature. These stories, and the earliest tragedies of Ibsen, made their appearance in a society which had successfully starved the romantic parts of literature, and in which nothing fresh or brilliant was even looked for. In the much more cultivated and literary neighbour-country, Denmark, to whose population the Norwegian poets had to look for their main audience, letters were far from being in so abject a state. Yet here the ideal was one of delicacy and polish, rather than of native freshness. The eminent Danish critic, Georg Brandes, whose youth was identical with the first successes of Björnson, has told us how strange and almost repulsive the earliest peasant stories of the latter seemed to him, fresh from the harmony of Oehlenschläger's tragedies and the piercing sweetness of the exquisite lyrics of Hertz. This new thing from Norway seemed rough, harsh, unripe. It took some little time for this odour of the mountain juniper to captivate the nerves of the Copenhageners.

The peasant-romance was a creation of the middle of the present century. At the very close of his life, in 1839, Immermann wrote *Der Oberhof*, a little story which is not merely likely to survive his romantic tragedies and novels, but which began a new order of literature. The *Dorfgeschichten* of the Alsatian Alexander Weill followed in 1841, and those of Auerbach in 1843.

The repute of these German stories awakened in George Sand the desire to emulate them, and led immediately to the composition of *Jeanne* and *La Mars au Diable*. In Switzerland " Jeremias Gotthelf " (Albert Bitzius) followed in the same path. Within a single decade after the publication of Immermann's *Der Oberhof* most could grow the flower for all had got the seed. Fritz Reuter, from his home in the wilds of Mecklenburg, was sending forth humorous and pathetic tales, in the patois of his locality, a series which was to culminate in *Ut mine stromtid*. In this class of literature, the romantic tendencies of the time, by a very natural reaction, turned from the splendours of aristrocratic mediævalism, from the magnificent sorrows of burgraves and châtelaines, to the incidents which diversified the simple annals of the poor. It was a recrudescence of the idyl, in its most primitive form ; a recapture of the early charm of that bucolic poetry which had become so vapid in the pursuit of china gods and Dresden shepherdesses.

It is interesting, perhaps, to note the existence of this school of rural pastoral flourishing throughout Europe in the forties, and to recognise Björnson's kinship with these writers of *dorfgeschichten*. But, as a matter of fact, their work, though it may lead up to his, does not explain it. Björnson has stated, I believe, that when he began to compose his *bonde-novellen* no page of Auerbach or George Sand had ever met his eyes. This might be quite true, and yet their influence might have given his genius the start-word. When a certain tendency is in the air, there is a sympathy which directs more surely than knowledge. From the spring of 1854 until the time when he first became known as a novelist, Björnson was living by miscellaneous contributions, mostly reviews of books, to the newspapers of Christiania. In this way, the general movement of literature could not fail to have swept him along in its tide, and if he read no George Sand or Fritz Reuter he must, at least, have read about them. The last-mentioned, at all events, was the object of the keen curiosity of Björnson's intimate friend, the poet Vinje.

His peasant-stories, however, in any case, are quite unlike Auerbach's. The key to their comprehension is to be found in the phrase which has already been quoted—the novelist was observing the peasant in the light of the saga. The greatest national inheritance of the Scandinavians, and particularly of the Norwegians, is their body of heroic sagas. These, as is well known, are the prose epics written in Iceland from the ninth century onward, from what is called the Sögu-öld or Saga-Age, down to the historical period of Sturla and his friends, in the twelfth century. The term "saga," often so loosely used, covers all in the way of romance, poem, chronicle, biography, written in the ancient language of the North during the splendid age of Icelandic supremacy. Whenever modern Scandinavian literature has been healthy, it has shown its vigour by a return to these heroic sources of national life. During the long decay of letters, the treasures of the saga were neglected, almost lost, wholly misinterpreted. The successive revivers of the poetry of Scandinavia, from Evald to Oehlenschläger, from Franzén to Geijer and Tegnér, have gone to the heroes and demigods of the semi-mythical antiquity of Iceland, for the springs of their inspiration.

But everything tends to fossilise in our world of decay, and the mode in which the Danish and Swedish poets of the beginning of the present century regarded the sagas, exquisitely fresh as it seemed to their own contemporaries, soon became conventional in the imitators of their style. The two acknowledged masterpieces of modern saga-writing, the *Helge* of Oehlenschläger and the *Frithiof* of Tegnér, with all their charm and vigour, are oligarchical romances, by no means unaffected by the vogue of Sir

Walter Scott, and they transfer the elements of ancient Scandinavian legend into a modern atmosphere much as Scott has transferred those of Scottish history into his long narrative poems. Oehlenschläger did more than this, for he was pre-eminently a tragic dramatist of a high if not of the highest class, but even Oehlenschläger's tragedies admit qualities of sentiment and composite reflection foreign to the bare simplicity of the sagas.

Let us now consider the form and substance of *Thrond*, the story with which Björnson, in 1856, began his career as a writer. It is written in curt, unadorned sentences, almost in monosyllables, and with a simplicity of manner which is the product, not of artlessness (for modern artlessness is florid and voluble) but of the most careful art. The tale is one of the purest Norwegian isolation. A man called Alf lives alone in a hut in the mountains, scarcely speaking to his sparse and distant neighbours. He is called "Alf of the Woods." One day he comes down to the village and is married to a young girl as shy as himself. Months pass, and Alf's wife appears carrying a babe for the priest to baptise, and then they disappear again in the mountain woodlands.

This child is the boy Thrond. - One Christmas

night his father breaks the silence by telling
Thrond a wild fairy-story, about the Devil; and
imagination wakens in the boy. Later on, a
wandering fiddler, starved and worn, dies in
the house of Alf, and the violin is left there,
unclaimed. Melodies begin to surge in the
boy's brain, fostered by the quiet of the woodlands, by the legends that his father tells him
and by the airs that his mother sings to him,
by the mystery and magic of the long Norwegian twilights. Thrond becomes a mighty
fiddler, and the desire comes over him—throttling,
shaking, thrilling him—the mad longing to take
his fiddle in his hand and walk over the hills
and far away, down into the wonderful valleys
of fairy-land.

At last Thrond has a chance. He is invited
to come to the nearest village, and play at a
wedding. From morning to evening he practises,
and all night long he cannot sleep because of the
new *slaater* (wedding-marches) which come to
him in his half-dreams. He starts off at day-
break, and the descriptive genius of Björnson is
here seen at its height, already—full-grown at
birth—in the ravishing pages which tell of
Thrond's walk through the forest till he sees
the village far below him, clinging like a cloud
against the mountain-side. Dancing to the lilt

of the airs that bubble in his brain, the boy
approaches the church, and he gazes with
astonishment at the human beings whom he now
sees clustered for the first time in his life. But
his triumph is marred ; a vision clouds his eyes ;
he begins to play and all the notes are jarred
together. He finds himself lying out on the
lonely brae-side, his fiddle flung before him.
He cuts the strings in passion, but his mother
hangs above him, weeping, and will tempt him
homeward. Then a great fear comes over him ;
he holds up the broken instrument between his
mother and himself. "No, Mother! no! home
again I will not go, till I can play what I have
seen to-day!"

The allegory is translucent. It is one to
which, in different shapes, Björnson often recurs.
The poet is one who, in the solitudes of life,
surrounded by no favourable influences but those
of nature, yearns with a passionate longing to
make music for mankind, to march at the head
of a procession of his fellows, to lead the way
in some wild adventure and storm the ports of
fairy-land. But, always, when he has his first
opportunity, it is to meet with disappointment
and disenchantment that he has come so far.
The violin which has so long bewitched him
betrays him in the final hour, and, amid the

laughter of those whom he has been ambitious to lead, he is thrown upon the mountain-side and deserted. But, in spite of disillusion, there is no possibility of return for him to the old conventions and respectabilities. He has to stay in the harsh world, and learn to master the instrument that has befooled him, before he can betake himself again to the country of his childhood.

Of realism, as we now conceive it, there was little in such a story as *Thrond*. But of reality there was a great deal. Here, for the first time, the imaginative quality in the character of the peasant was truly and consistently depicted. *Thrond*, too, was but a sketch; it was quickly followed by pictures conceived in the same style, but executed with greater elaboration. *A Dangerous Wooing*, a wild little story, belongs to 1856; *The Bear Hunter* to 1857. But to the world at large Björnson was first revealed by the romance of *Synnöve Solbakken*, 1857; *Arne* followed in 1858; *A Happy Boy* in 1860. After a long pause, during which Björnson was occupied with other species of literary enterprise, *The Fisher Maiden* was published in 1868, and *The Wedding-March* closed the series in 1872. In these stories a Björnson can be studied who was for a long time the only one recognised through Europe, and who even yet is the best known, the author of pastoral prose-sagas of modern life which have not been surpassed for naïveté, freshness and sprightly delicacy.

The form of these stories had a peculiarity which is not apparent to a foreign reader, even in the very best translation. As we are often reminded, Norway possesses no language of her own, but employs that of the Danes. The Norse tongue can be spoken of merely as we speak of those who talk Scotch. But, as must always be the case when the inhabitants of a large mountainous country use the speech of a small group of flat islands and peninsulas, the Danish vocabulary is insufficient for the needs of the Norwegians, and a multitude of dictionary words are unknown out of Norway. This fuller vocabulary, however, was not enough to give isolation to the Norwegians, and about the time that Björnson began to write, the first attempt was made to create a real *Norsk*, a veritable language for Norway. The leader in this attempt was a man of great learning and ability, Ivar Aasen, who still survives ; he formed with remarkable ingenuity a sort of normal language based on the local dialects and the ancient speech of the country. It was his intention that this *bonde-maal* or peasant-language should supersede the

Danish spoken in the towns, and should become the written language of Norway.

The earliest publications of Ivar Aasen date back to 1848, but it was in 1853, in his *Pröver af Landsmaalet* ("Specimens of the Popular Language ") that he drew general attention to his scheme. To show the poets how to use their new instrument, Aasen published in 1855 a lyrical comedy, *Ervingen*, entirely in the composite language. He had many followers, and, in particular, Björnson's friend Vinje threw himself heart and soul into the *Landsmaal;* his devotion to it, indeed, has obscured the genius of one of the truest poets of modern Scandinavia. Björnson, fortunately, was saved from such extravagance, but the danger was at one time very great. Ibsen, from the first, refused to cut himself off from Europe by any participation in this " monkey-jabber," as he calls it in *Peer Gynt*, but Björnson was not at all sure that it did not behove a Norse patriot to write only in the tongue of his countrymen. He even translated one of his short stories, *A Dangerous Wooing* (" Et farligt Frieri " in Danish), into *bondemaal* as " Ej faarleg Friing ; " but there, happily, he stayed his hand. Nor, when in 1858 Vinje began to issue his newspaper *Dölen* (" The Peasant "), written entirely in Aasen's artificial idiom—a journal which Vinje contrived to support for ten years—did Björnson do more than approve and encourage. Sorely tempted and attracted, the greater poet continued to write in Danish.

It has been recorded, however, by Brandes that the earliest peasant-novels were far from being received at first with enthusiasm in Copenhagen. They were diametrically opposed to what the Danish public was accustomed to appreciate, and there was something foreign and odd about their diction which repelled fastidious readers. The fact is that though Björnson had not consented to join the *maalstrævere*—as they were called, the Strivers for a Language—he had been very strongly affected by their investigations into the traditional tongue of the peasants. He had at once observed that the popular dialects, in the depths of the great valleys of Norway, had preserved not a little of the resonance and pre-cision of the ancient *norræna*, the language of his beloved sagas. While he was too sensible a man to fling away the speech of the educated masses of his countrymen for a sentimental faddist's dream of a national tongue, he yet could not persuade himself to relinquish words, phrases, grammatical forms which were certainly not Danish, but which appealed to him by their picturesqueness or their local colour. It was the presence in his stories of so much that was odd and unfamiliar that puzzled the Copenhageners. We may consider for ourselves how extraordinary would seem to Londoners the language of Mr. Crockett or Mr. Barrie if we had not long been accustomed to Scotticisms in imaginative literature.

Any prejudice, however, which the somewhat exotic diction of these peasant-novels may have caused at first, has long ago ceased to exist. They brought with them the ineffable freshness of the remote Norwegian landscape, of the vast ravines, fledged with pine-trees, the long sonorous cascades, the melancholy lakes holding their dim mirrors up among the mountains, the salt fjords winding their oceanic waters so strangely in the very heart of the woodland. And with all this, in sequestered and scattered villages, whose soul, as Björnson says, is the church-spire, they suggested the hard Calvinism of the North, the austere biblical protestantism, externally so cold, holding underneath its crust such burning possibilities of passion. With all this, a mode of artistic procedure far more minute and realistic than we were then accustomed to, Björnson was unconsciously working in the same direction as the great Russians were. It is not uninteresting to recollect that the year which saw the publication of *Arne* saw that of Tourganieff's *Assja*, and that Tolstoi's *Three Deaths* belongs to 1859.

In Björnson's peasant-novels, the freshness and the verisimilitude of the conversations is above praise. A distinguished French critic, M. Ernest Tissot, has compared the *bonde-novellen* in this respect with the best work of Flaubert, " so prodigious is the art by which is reproduced, in a concise brevity, the talk of the peasant, with its apparent aimlessness, its reticence, its pleonasms, its frivolities and its tiresome repetitions. The personages of Björnson have upon their lips, not phrases learned out of some comedy, but simple, affectionate, obvious commonplaces, such as a phonograph might transmit to us." As examples of the marvellous power of the author in this respect, we may point to the conversation at the church-door in the eighth chapter of *Synnöve Solbakken*, and the chatter in the hay-field in the tenth chapter of *A Happy Boy*.

It will probably be conceded that the earliest of these stories are the best. Even *A Happy Boy*, entertaining as it is, strikes a moralising note in its hortatory optimism which is not so pure a delight as the development of the savage beauty of Thorbjörn's character in *Synnöve Solbakken*, or of the dreamer and enthusiast in

Arne. These two stories seem to me to be almost perfect ; they have an enchanting lyrical quality, without bitterness or passion, which I look for elsewhere in vain in the prose literature of the second half of the century. *The Fisher Maiden* is not so simple or direct. Interesting as it is, as a study of the processes by which a young woman of genius arrives at a command of her own resources, it is injured, as a simple peasant-story, by the incursion of foreign elements, by an excess of theological subtlety, by a modernity, in fact, which disturbs the harmony of the parts. Finally, *The Wedding-March* is a trifle ; it is one of F.dvard Grieg's *Norse Dances* translated into words. It recurs to the old manner which Björnson had invented twenty-five years before, and it repeats it with agility, but nothing is added, while certainly something is lost of freshness and sincerity. It is by *Arne* and by *Synnöve Solbakken*, two little masterpieces of the purest water, that the Björnson of the *bonde-novellen* lives and will continue to live.

III

While, however, Björnson was observing the peasant in the light of the saga, in his prose-stories, he was busily engaged all the time in creating the saga in the light of the peasant, in what he called his national dramas or *folke-stykker*. These latter form a section of his work which is little known to readers outside Scandinavia, but which demands full consideration from the critic. For fifteen years of his youth, Björnson did not despair of creating out of the heroic materials of ancient Norwegian history a popular series of plays which should appeal to all ages and all classes alike, and which should awaken a practical longing for vigour and beauty in the national life. Very similar, and not less vain, had been the efforts of the " Young England " party with us some dozen years earlier.

In the case of Norway, there was the saga, vaguely so described, the mass of noble ancient chronicle, full of the primal elements of personal courage, rapid, decisive action and the pathos of vast exploits vainly accomplished. This storehouse of poetic and dramatic inspiration had, indeed, not remained untouched. Pre-eminently, it had been entered and ransacked by the greatest poet of Denmark, by Adam Gottlob Oehlenschläger, whose long series of magnificent national tragedies, produced between 1805 and 1845, testify to his instinct for saga-treasure. The influence of Oehlenschläger, however, had begun to wane before his death in 1850; his later tragedies were rhetorical, lax and cold, and with Heiberg and Hertz, as the rulers of poetic taste in Denmark, reference to the saga became a sort of stigma, an evidence of bad taste.

It was therefore a proof alike of originality and of that curious involuntary parallelism which has marked them through life, that the two unknown Norwegian poets who were to become so famous, each started his serious career with a saga-drama—Ibsen with *The Feast at Solhoug* in 1856, Björnson with *Between the Battles* ("Mellem Slagene") in 1857, each play written, I believe, in the early part of 1855. We have here to do only with Björnson's drama, which is a little piece in a single act. Civil war is raging in Norway between King Magnus and King Sverre, and in a mountain-hut, between two engagemeuts, Sverre appears, disguised as Oysteijn, one of the scouts of Magnus. The object of Sverre in this masquerade remains obscure, although a long and vigorous soliloquy towards the end of the play is intended to explain that, with a public character for devilry and love of bloodshed, he is really longing for peace and a mild Saturnian reign, and to show that, "between the battles," the wildest tyrants can be lovers of their kind. But the psychological interest of the piece, which is considerable, centres around the figure of Inga, a woman who has been torn from the house of her father, Thorkel, by a wild mountain-man, Halvard Gjæla, whom she loves ; her love for this father of her child, however, is less than that she feels for her own father, or, at least, the one constantly disturbs the other, so that she is torn with nostalgia and unrest. The magnanimity of Sverre restores her father to her, and completes the family group. The elements of several of Björnson's favourite theories may be perceived in the working out of *Between the Battles,* a dramatic sketch which lacks coherence, but is full of life, of freshness, of an audacious method in the treatment of history.

Of the form of *Between the Battles* something must be said. As in the story called *Thrond* Björnson created, at the first attempt, a kind of tale hitherto unattempted, a kind, too, which he would not succeed in modifying as he proceeded, so in this earliest and somewhat crude theatrical sketch, he struck forth a new species of dramatic form, of which he was destined to make repeated and indeed constant use. *Between the Battles,* although a contribution to heroic drama, was written in prose, and that of a kind distinctly novel in character, terse, direct and personal. There was a total absence of the rhetoric hitherto deemed requisite for tragedy, an absence of the *cliches* of tragic poetry. In all this, Björnson was a serious innovator, and the result is that, to this day, this production of his crude youth may be read, without any sense of incongruity, among his dramatic writings.

:. The same can hardly be said of his next dramatic effort, the three-act heroic drama of *Halte-Hulda* (" Lame Hulda "). Here, his courage as to form gave way, and he retreated from the nervous prose which had suited his purpose and temper so well, back to a soft blank verse of the kind approved of by Heiberg and Hertz. Perhaps it is for this reason that Björnson has not kept *Halte-Hulda*—which can only be obtained in a dim edition of 1859, printed at Bergen—in the series of his works ; it may be that he is conscious of its juvenility. It is, indeed, scarcely worthy of him, or of the high promise of *Between the Battles;* but it contains some grim and some lamentable scenes, all of which are full of power. The savage passion of Hulda is drawn in traits worthy of Racine, and with an antique barbaric strenuousness which is really remarkable. This little drama, too, contains some charming lyrics. But if, as would seem to be the case, the author has excluded it from the series of his living works, his action is on the whole justifiable. *Halte-Hulda* has masterly pages in it, but it is far from being a masterpiece.

If a sign be needed of the rapidity with which the genius of Björnson developed as he approached his thirtieth year, it is found in the difference between the tragedy of *King Sverre*, which he wrote in Rome in the spring of 1861, and the trilogy of *Sigurd Slembe* ("Sigurd the Bastard"), which he wrote partly in Munich, partly in the Tyrol, in the following year. *King Sverre* has never been reprinted, and is now practically inaccessible ; I am forced to speak of it from a memory which is nearly twenty years old, for I have been unable to re-read it for the purposes of the present study. But the impression I retain is one of comparative feebleness and incoherence, and the poet has, no doubt, acted wisely in suppressing it. *Sigurd Slembe*, on the other hand, is one of his most emphatic successes. In all the various repertory of Björnson, there is perhaps no single work in which so high a level of technical excellence is aimed at, and at the same time so harmonious and dignified a result obtained. Looking over the twenty-five or thirty volumes which Björnson has presented to the public, there is probably not one from which, in Landor's phrase, there is less for criticism " to pare away " than from *Sigurd Slembe*.

This marvellous poem is, what none of Björnson's other essays in the same direction succeed in being, a complete saga in dramatic form. The peculiar simplicity and strenuous passion of the old semi-historical chronicles of Iceland are here preserved to the full, and there is added to them a modern complexity in the evolution of character. The author has called *Sigurd Slembe* a trilogy, but it really consists of two long plays, introduced by a dramatic prologue. In the last-mentioned of these, Sigurd is presented to us, a powerful, handsome, turbulent youth, full of energy and ambition. His gifts, however, which are various and brilliant, are rendered almost useless to him in a country so feudal as Norway in the twelfth century, because he knows not of what clan he is ; he is Slembe, the Fatherless, perhaps the Bastard. Hence, in the opening scene, in the Cathedral of Stavanger, in front of the statue of St. Olaf, he forces from his mother the confession of the name of his father. Ready to expire of shame, the poor woman reveals at last that King Magnus Barefoot was her lover. But Sigurd rises hopeful and unabashed. At length he knows from what race he comes ; he is the Fatherless One no longer. He breaks away from mother and friends, and the wild spirit of adventure sends him panting over the seas to southward, mad to achieve a name and to return to claim the throne of Norway.

In the next play, " Sigurd's Second Flight," we find the hero stranded on the coast of Caithness in the shrunken court of the exiled earl of Orkney. This earl, Harald, is a sickly and abnormal boy, ruled over by his mother, Helga, and her violent and intriguing sister, Frakerk. Harald has no ambition ; he feels death approaching, and asks no more than to be at rest among his dreams ; his life is tortured by the schemes and the wranglings of the women of his household. These ladies, on their part, are in despair at his indolence, and, in their anxiety, they turn to this magnificent Norseman, this grave and mysterious Sigurd who has arrived in their palace nobody knows whence, as to a stronghanded man who may be hired to espouse their cause. They have an orphan niece, Audhild, who is one of Björnson's subtlest and finest female creations, and this girl falls in love with Sigurd. The Norwegian, of course, succeeds completely and directly in the campaign against Orkney, but the young Earl, on whom the burden of responsible existence has grown to be too heavy a weight, commits suicide by wearing a shirt poisoned by his aunt Frakerk for another pretender, and Sigurd, rejecting the crown which now lies at his hand, passes out to sea again, unable to endure any longer the intrigues and horrors of the dreadful house of Caithness. He tears himself from the arms of Audhild in a scene of extraordinary beauty and passion.

Then follows the closing play, " Sigurd's Return Home." He comes back to the court of his half-brother, King Harald Gille, in Bergen, with the same hopes and illusions that accompanied him when he left Norway ; once more he strives to grasp his fate, and once more vexation of spirit is all his reward. The close of this play contains two enchanting passages, each of which reaches Björnson's high-water mark in purely poetical composition—one being the scene between Sigurd and the Finn Girl, the other Sigurd's sublime final soliloquy, beginning, " The Danes desert me ! the battle is lost ! Here— and no further ! " The whole trilogy closes with the song of the Crusaders, while listening to whom, all his worldly hopes being broken, Sigurd leans his weary head once more against the bosom of his aged mother.

In 1872, Björnson published yet another and a final saga-drama, *Sigurd Jorsalfar* (" Sigurd the Crusader "). A Jorsalfar was a man who performed the pilgrimage to Jerusalem or Jórsalir.

This is a brilliant little sketch rather than a carefully wrought dramatic poem ; it runs on the clashing between two royal brothers, Eystejn, the modern man of progress, and Sigurd, the type of a sensuous mediæval warrior. Sigurd picks a quarrel with Eystejn, and will take as the instrument of his revenge, Borghild, the fairest woman in Norway, who has long been promised marriage by King Eystejn, and who is shamed by his delay. A scene in which Sigurd suddenly presents himself, splendid and masculine, with the gold and silk of the East upon him, in the moated grange of this Norse Mariana, and offers her his hand and a seat on the throne by his side, is in the dramatist's best manner. No other page of *Sigurd Jorsalfar* is quite intelligible enough or congruous enough to be praised without reservation.

In all the saga-plays of Björnson a type constantly reappears, in which it is not difficult to perceive the poet's portrait of his own shadow thrown huge and vague upon the mists of history. He is Sverre, the man with the devil in him cast out as a disturber of Norway, yet consumed with a love of his country ; he is Sigurd the Bastard, his patristic birthright denied, his claim to serve his people repudiated, his warmest ambitions foiled ; he is Sigurd Jorsalfar, sick and mad until he learns the lesson that moral health is only found in the modest pursuance of civic duties. These plays were the expression of a stormy egotism, which contained nothing ignoble or small, but much which was disturbing and experimental. Hence, with the one exception of *Sigurd Slembe*, which is a very noble piece of sustained writing, the saga-dramas are curious and interesting, rather than satisfactory. They might be pages out of Hamlet's commonplace book, scenes hastily scrawled to test the capacity of his players. Björnson's ambition in writing them was to found with them a national Norwegian drama, but on the stage their theatrical limitations become instantly obvious. *Sigurd Slembe*, indeed, in spite of its attractions, has succeeded but once in appearing before the footlights ; in November 1869, the Meiningen company acted it in full, but were never tempted to repeat their experiment. When it is considered that Björnson, for a great part of the time in which these essays at folk-drama were being made, was manager and director of a theatre, it is strange that he never contrived to bring his own poetry and the stage into practical inter-relation.

One great theatrical success he enjoyed, indeed, and to that it is now time to give a few words. *Mary Stuart in Scotland*, which was written partly in Bergen and partly in Christiania in the summer of 1864, and published at the close of that year, is an historical play treated in the same way as saga is treated in *Sigurd Slembe*, that is to say, mainly with an eye to the psychological development of character. In the long line of dramas dealing with the history of the beautiful and unfortunate queen, a series beginning with the *Écossaise* of Montchrestien, and closing, for the present, with Mr. Swinburne's fervid trilogy, the drama of Björnson takes a prominent place. It preceded the publication of *Chastelard* by a few months, and the two poems so far resemble each other, that each was a bold attempt to reject the conventional (or sub-Schillerian) method of treating such a theme, and to reproduce the actual temperament of the latest French Renaissance.

The poet himself was pleased with his work. He wrote long afterwards, " if the people who animate my *Mary Stuart* are not living beings, then I have never succeeded in drawing men and women with blood in their veins." For some reason, unknown to me, three years were allowed to pass before *Mary Stuart* was put on the boards. When this was at last done, its success was instant and assured, and it has continued to be the most popular of recent romantic dramas on the Norwegian stage.

Björnson's Mary Stuart, however, is not convincing. She moves gracefully and fatally through the play, but Mr. Swinburne's portrait of her has spoiled an English reader for a mild Teutonic shadow of her passion. On the other hand, Björnson has drawn Bothwell boldly and well, and by carefully studying the pietistic fanaticism of his own land and age, he has succeeded in creating a plausible, if not a very Scotch, John Knox.

IV

As a poet in the English sense, that is to say as a writer in verse, Björnson has not been prolific. Only one of his dramas, *Halte-Hulda*, is versified throughout, in a form adopted from that of the Danish tragic poets of the beginning of the century. In the summer of 1870 he collected his lyrical writings into a slender volume of *Poems and Songs* (" Digte og Sange "), which he has enlarged in successive editions ; it is the only collection of the kind which he has made. Björnson's solitary poem of any length is the epical romance of *Arnljot Gelline*, also published in 1870. Into many of his novels and his dramas he has introduced songs which have a great charm of melody and sentiment ; most of these are to be found re-printed in the current edition of *Digte og Sange*. Like all recent Scandinavian poets, much of his lyrical work consists of verses of occasion—lines written for weddings, for funerals, for anniversa-ries, for deputations, for bazaars, addressed to famous friends, or composed for the feasts or torch-processions of the students. These pieces are apt to be of ephemeral interest, especially for a stranger. Yet in many cases Björnson has contrived to throw the charm of his impassioned optimism into the strophes.

He seems to be most fortunate, however, in two directions, as a song-writer and as a resus-citator of the old heroic staves of the Icelanders. His songs are often of a delicious freshness, and of a natural music which defies the translator. Of his political lyrics one, at least, *Ja, vi elsker dette landet* ("Yes ! we love this our country !"), has achieved the most complete popular success, and in the musical setting made for it by Nord-raak, has become the national hymn of Norway. Of the Eddaic or saga poems of Björnson, *Berg-liot* is universally acknowledged to be the finest. In this noble unrhymed ode, which in the volume and rapidity of its movement reminds an English reader of the *Boadicea* of Tennyson, Bergliot, the widow of Ejnar Tambarskelve, laments the killing of that hero and of his only son, and while raving over their dead bodies, urges the peasants on to the revenge of their chieftains. The poem opens with a wild volubility of indignation, passes into a crescendo of rage and impotent fury, and then sinks by fits and starts to the melody of hopeless grief. *Bergliot* is one of the masterpieces of modern Scandinavian poetry, and its varied gamut of dramatic passion makes it the favourite exercise of ambitious reciters.

Of the fifteen cantos or " songs " of which the romance of *Arnljot Gelline* is composed, the fifth, " Arnljot's Longing for the Sea," is the most imaginative and distinguished. Many of the other divisions are simply lyrics of a more or less romantic character, little connected with the story of the hero, but the general impression which the poem leaves is one similar to that of the saga-dramas. Arnljot is a viking, torn by conflicting ambitions and responsibilities, always suffering and sinning, till he finds rest at last, slain in the service of St. Olaf at the great battle of Stiklestad.

V

Between 1864 and 1874, that is to say between the ages of thirty-two and forty-two,

Björnson displayed a slackening of the intellectual forces which was most remarkable in a man of his energy. In the face of the prolific production of the last twenty years of his life, it is curious indeed to look back upon the long period when it seemed as though his talent had all run to seed, his early vigour and fertility become prematurely exhausted. The reasons for this withdrawal, however, were mainly political. The death of Frederick VII. of Denmark was the event which closed Björnson's early career as a poet ; he finished *Mary Stuart in Scotland*, and then he sat down to observe what was going to happen in Scandinavian history. Like Ibsen, upon whom the war of 1864 produced a similar blighting influence, he was a zealous pan-Scandinavian, and believed it to be the duty of the united kingdoms to come to the help of Denmark against Germany. He wrote to Hans Christian Andersen (on the 6th of March, 1864) : " I am occupying my thoughts with prosaic theatrical business, for, at such a crisis as this, poetical composition is not to be thought of." All through 1864 he was failing to make terms with the Christiania Theatre, but matters were finally settled to his satisfaction, and on New Year's Day, 1865, he was installed there as " scenic and artistic manager."

With politics and with the practical management of this house Björnson was actively engaged, the latter being constantly disturbed by bitter discussions as to the limits and scope of his managerial responsibility, until June 1867, when he resigned the post. Meanwhile, he was giving to the newspaper press what was meant for mankind, and expending his best intellectual energies in journalistic polemics. In March 1866 he became the editor of a newspaper, the *Norsk Folkebled*, which had been founded with the idea of excluding political discussion, but which under Björnson's editorship speedily became the hottest of radical organs. To give himself a still freer hand, in the autumn of 1869 Björnson bought this paper for himself, and carried it on until the close of 1871. At the same time, he entered with zeal into public political life, as a speaker and agitator ; while in 1871 he began to give lectures in various towns of Norway and Sweden, thus commencing a department of work for which he has since shown great aptitude. His noble appearance, the fulness and resonance of his well-trained voice, the virile ardour of his delivery, combine to make Björnson an ideal lecturer. The end of all this restlessness, and of the social discomforts which his political activity brought upon him, was a brusque determination to follow

Ibsen into exile. He left Norway in the early part of 1873, and spent two years and a half in the south of Europe. The result of this quiet period, coming at the close of so much stir and bustle, was to reawaken in him the creative instincts which had so long been dormant. Björnson, in 1874, became once more, what he has remained, an imaginative writer.

During these ten years of quiescence, it is not to be supposed that he was entirely barren, but most of his compositions might as well have been left unwritten. If that be too severe a judgment, they were, at least, in the main, imitations of his old self, efforts that showed no progress or revival. *The Fisher Maiden* of 1868, and *The Bridal March* of 1873, were novels which added little to the prestige of the author of *Arne; Sigurd Jorsalfar* in 1872 and even the epic poem of *Arnljot Gelline* merely continued with dignity and in a satisfactory style the saga-manner already amply indicated by the previous heroic dramas, while the earlier and far fresher portion of the last-mentioned poem had been written years before the Danish war. Björnson was waiting, dreaming, preparing for the great change to come over his spirit, and the sign that this change had come was the simultaneous appearance of *The Editor* and *A Bank-ruptcy* in 1875.

At the close of this transitional period Björn-son produced two specimens of fiction, neither of which can conveniently be classed with any of his other work. Of these *Captain Mansana* is an impassioned episode of the war of Italian in-dependence, written in Aulestad, indeed, but full of memories and impressions of the south. Of much greater importance is the little novel of *Magnhild*, in which the poet is distinctly seen to start, with somewhat faltering steps, upon a new path. He is here visibly affected by French models, and by the methods of the naturalists, but he is trying to combine them with his own simpler traditions of rustic realism. Björnson was accused of an immoral tendency in writing *Magnhild*, and with desiring to uphold the prin-ciples of free love. He indignantly rebuffed the charge, which was made unintelligently enough. What he certainly was suggesting in the novel was a greater respect for the essential sanctity of the marriage tie and a less superstitious regard for the merely conventional and unreal bond. He distinguishes between a formal and a real marriage, and suggests that if the social union is founded on a falsehood, it should be broken as soon as possible. The reader, more accustomed to strong situations to-day than he was in 1877, must make what he can of the relation of Mrs. Bang to Tande.

The fact is—from the critical side, and this affects the moral—that *Magnhild* is an irregular and imperfect composition. The author felt himself greatly moved by fermenting ideas and ambitions which he had not completely mastered ; he expressed his sensations as clearly as he could, in the twilight of his perception of their relative values. The result is that, side by side with passages of character-painting which are full of power and delicacy, there is much in the texture of *Magnhild* which is vague and unreal. The mysticism of many of the sentiments is cloudy and even somewhat morbid, and there is a kind of uncomfortable discrepancy between the scene and the style, a breath of Paris and the boulevards blowing through the pine-trees of a puritanical Norwegian village. The reader's interest is concentrated on the three figures of Bang and his wife, and the amorous young musician. In writing *Magnhild* Björnson had not yet mastered the art of crowding his canvas with groups of living modern men and women. But the book is a most interesting link between the early peasant-stories and the great novels of his latest period.

VI

In the career of Björnson, as in that of Ibsen, a very large place is filled by the succession of " social " dramas in prose, undertaken during middle life. Curiously enongh, as Ibsen, in 1869, produced *The Young Men's Union*, which was utterly unlike anything he had previously written, dimly foreshadowing the stronger prose-plays of the future, so in Björnson's repertory, too, there is one comedy which is a sort of petrel flying before the storm of severe realistic dramas with a purpose. *The Newly-Married Couple* (" De Nygifte "), which it is difficult to put anywhere else, may, then, be included in this section, although, in its pretty optimism, it is sufficiently unlike the sturdy plays which will be here associated with it.

In the spring of 1865 Björnson was appointed manager of the Christiania Theatre, and his conduct of the house had the result of immediately improving its finances. In Norway he wrote in the summer, but published in Copenhagen in November, the little play of which we are now speaking. He did not bring out *The Newly-Married Couple* at his own house first, but let it be earliest judged at the Royal Theatre in Copenhagen, where on the 23rd of November, 1865, it enjoyed a triumphant success. Nearly thirty years have passed, and still this little comedy is a stock-piece at every Scandinavian theatre. It is, of all Björnson's dramatic productions, that which has pleased the greatest number of play-goers. It is also the smallest; it is nothing more ambitious than a little sentimental comedy of manners in two acts.

In later years, the complaint has often been heard that Ibsen gets in front of Björnson, and develops new ideas a few weeks earlier than his rival and fair enemy. But here, for once, it cannot be doubted that Björnson was well ahead of the author of *A Doll's House* in his study of the awakening to responsibility of a girl whose mind and heart have been stunted by too shel-tered and indulgent a training. Laura has been told by her father and mother, whose only child she is, that she is to marry Axel, and she does so cheerfully. Axel is to live with the parents, and it is to be an ideal household. But Laura has developed no love for any one but her father and mother; their needs, her anxieties about them, fill all the corners of her soul, and if the inte-rests of Axel clash with these duties, the husband must be sacrificed instantly, completely, without a thought.

Very amusingly, and yet tenderly, the condition of things is revealed in the opening scene at breakfast. But Axel has no notion of being a mere fly on the wheel of parental felicity. He perceives that he has made a mistake in acquiescing in an arrangement which seemed to promise so much serene enjoyment. He sees that he is in danger of never awakening the love of his child-wife for himself. The parents—excellent folk, but too yielding—take his view of the situation, and consent to be banished from Laura, who has to face the loss of them, and isolation with the husband who is still a stranger to her heart. A year later the curtain rises on Axel's house; Laura is still unconsoled and unforgiving. But love for the patient and considerate husband is struggling in her heart with the offended dignity of the daughter, and as the events which are skilfully marshalled in the second act unwind themselves, her heart is more and more fully awakened. She learns to love her husband for his own sake, and she is rewarded by reunion with the old parents from whom, until the new birth of duty is strong enough to bear the stress of their presence, she has been carefully separated. *The Newly-Married Couple* is a quaint little piece, very Scandinavian in feeling, not devoid of obvious faults of construction, but so homely, odd and direct that it has always gone straight to the heart of the people.

The real series of social dramas, however, began nine years later. Björnson had become more and more absorbed in political interests and agitations, and these are reflected in the plays which occupied him from 1874 onwards. He had found life in Norway intolerable to him, although at this very moment he was in treaty for the purchase of Aulestad, the property in Gausdal which has for nearly twenty years been his home. In February 1873 he started for the south, proceeding leisurely through Sweden, and he was not seen in Norway again until June 1875. These two years of exile were fruitful in a poetical sense; he wrote much, and he wrote with an unparalleled force and novelty, as if, as the saying is, he had taken a new lease of life. Of the two plays which we have now to describe one, *The Editor* (" Redaktören ") was composed in Florence, the other, *A Bankruptcy*, partly in Rome and partly in the Tyrol.

In February 1875 *The Editor* was published in Copenhagen. It was rejected at the Royal Theatres of Denmark and Norway, but was performed, in a Swedish translation, in Stockholm and Gothenburg. Later on, in the month of April, it was acted, in defiance of the author's wishes, at a small theatre at Christiania, but the performance led to disturbances, and to an angry public controversy. From the first, justice was not done to *The Editor*, and it has never been appreciated. It was an attack on the egotism and passion of the press, and, as a matter of course, the journalists could not endure it. That Björnson should dare to attack this privileged class—the sacred priesthood of the close of the nineteenth century—was a vivid proof of his courage or at least of his temerity. But he was promptly punished for his audacity.

Yet, to an unprejudiced reader, *The Editor* seems an extremely interesting and original work, faulty, indeed, in its daring realism, but full of cleverness and verve. It is a sort of allegory, too, in which the author, half-unconsciously, gives himself the rôle of hero, and we see, with curiosity and amusement, what Björnson thought in 1874 of himself and the figure he cut in Norway. In the house of Eyje, a wealthy merchant, who is " moderate " and has always stood apart from politics, Halvdan Rejn is prospective son-in-law. He and his brother Harald are prominent members of the radical and free-thinking party, and are persecuted by the conservative press, particularly by the nameless

Editor of the leading reactionary newspaper. Harald Rejn (the old Radical party) has sunken into ill-health under the persecution ; Halvdan (that is to say Björnson) still holds his head erect; their elder brother, Haakon, a wealthy peasant in the country (the ancient spirit of Norwegian independence) is behind them both, and will come up to support them if the worst comes to the worst. Meanwhile the Editor makes their lives, and those of the Moderates, their friends, unbearable by his libellous attacks and daily insinuations.

Preposterous as it is in many ways—and especially in its close, where Harald breaks a blood-vessel and dies on reading an unparalleled article in the newspaper, and the Editor happens, as a passer-by, to be called in to carry his dead body to the bed—this play is full of vitality and a sort of mysterious vivacity. It can be read at a sitting, and can hardly be put down when it has been taken up. The second act is of a real theatrical ingenuity ; the action passes in a street of the city, in dense fog, and figures pass, strange and typical figures, laden with fate and intrigue. The conversations throughout are more sparkling than any which Björnson had written up to that date. It was a very remarkable experiment in dramatic composition, and one which was to lead its author and the literature of his country far.

If Björnson succeeded in ruffling the temper of his countrymen with *The Editor*, he immediately reconquered their suffrages with his extremely popular drama, *A Bankruptcy*.* The action of this piece is very simple. Tjælde is the head of a respectable Norwegian family, all the different members of which are presented to us in an interesting and sympathetic manner. But just as our affections are engaged, we learn that Tjælde stands on the edge of bankruptcy. For years before the opening of the play, with immense energy and skill he has been struggling to overcome the fate which is undermining his fortunes. In the second act, he is on the point of over-riding the storm once more by borrowing a large sum of money, and the interest centres around an elaborate conversation between Tjælde and a leading Christiania lawyer, Berant, a sort of commercial Mephistopheles, who proves to him

---

* According to Halvorsen and the other authorities, this play was not published until April 1875, *The Editor* having appeared in February of that year. But both plays must have been in type much earlier, for I was able to give some brief account of *The Editor* in the *Academy* for August 8, 1874, and although 1875 is the usual date on the title-page of the first edition of *A Bankruptcy*, the copy which lies before me, which reached me in the autumn before, bears 1874 on its title-page. Here seems to be a little bibliographical puzzle for some Spoelberch de Lovenjoul of the future to unravel.

that this loan will merely postpone the evil day
and make the final catastrophe more painful, and
who forces Tjælde to take the bold step of
declaring himself a bankrupt. When this is
done, and not till then, the circle of relations
and friends, relieved by the crash from the load
of their anxieties, can breathe again, and begin
to build up a future. The fourth act, after the
stress and mental agony of the other three, is as
refreshing as a cool evening after a lurid day of
tropic heat.

A Bankruptcy has been one of the most
popular of all Björnson's writings, but it cannot
be considered one of the most important. It
owes its popularity to a certain concession made
in it to the Teutonic family instinct, to the love
of the homely, the comfortable and the domestic.
Tjælde's business-affairs lack breadth of public
interest, and the field of his operations has
nothing national about it. No great public
calamity fills the background with its shadow,
and consequently the imagination is not deeply
moved. The blow will fall on the group of
indolent, good-natured, unoccupied persons who
are introduced to us in the first act, and our
interest in it is bounded by our interest in them.
That, indeed, is considerable, for the poet has
defined them so clearly and so genially, with a

humour so serene and a satire so unconscious of poison, that we share their anxieties as though they were personal friends. The second act of *A Bankruptcy* deserves higher praise than the rest of the play ; it is admirably conceived, and executed with a positive profusion of wit and vivacity. As the play proceeds, it becomes more and more German in its form ; we seem to be carried back a hundred years, to the family dramas of Iffland and Schröder.

M. Ernest Tissot, who calls *A Bankruptcy* "the tragi-comedy of money," compares it with *L'Avare* somewhat to the disadvantage of Molière. The theme was new, at all events, in Scandinavian literature, and in our own we have only to compare it with the *Money* of Lord Lytton to perceive the source of its lasting popularity. People love to see that represented on the stage which shows in the dramatist's mind a sympathy with their own secret preoccupations. But I cannot give *A Bankruptcy* so high a place as has been claimed for it by many critics of weight. The realism of the detail, which dazzled its earliest admirers, has become in the course of twenty years a matter of no extraordinary moment. In the light of Gerhard Hauptmann and Henri Becque it no longer seems effulgent. The drama is a very good, practical family drama of the Teutonic sort, but it is not a great imaginative masterpiece.

For several years Björnson was silent, and when he came forward again, it was with a very strange piece of dramatic work. *The King* ("Kongen"), when it was originally published in 1877, was received with a storm of disapproval. Few even of Björnson's admirers appreciated it at first.* It was of a startling originality of form, and it was pardonable, perhaps, for those who had acquired certain notions with regard to the poet's limitations, to resent seeing him suddenly fly outside of their circle, as an acrobat leaps abruptly far out of the reach of a ring of clowns, who try to hem him in. But, as one reads *The King* to-day, it is difficult to realise how so brilliant an intellectual extravaganza, so daring a political dream, should have failed to fascinate us from the first.

Not intended for the stage, *The King* is a series of realistic conversation scenes, inlaid in a double setting of ballet and masque. The curtain rises on a ball-room, where strange figures in dominos hurry about and whisper enigmas to one another. At length the King is

---

* The present writer was among them, and published certain remarks for which (being grown older and wiser) he would now do penance, in a white sheet.

divined pursuing a country-girl amongst the masquers, and the scene closes. It opens again on a mysterious Wagnerian pasturage, where, ringed about with clouds and wonders, three genii meet, and chant a long dramatic cantata in verse not less obscure than melodious. These choral interludes, which resemble in their fateful interweaving of staves the music or Eddaic poetry of the antiquity of the North, recur at the changes of scene, and with a muffled incantation close the play, which is otherwise in very direct prose of modern Norway.

Björnson has published few works more instinct with passion than *The King*. It bears some superficial relation to Victor Hugo's *Le Pape*, which had then been recently published, but it is less visionary, and comes more within the range of possibility. A young prince, of high intellectual gifts and trained among republicans, finds himself, by a series of deaths, raised unexpectedly to the throne. He is distressed by the incongruity of his position, of the system which he represents, and he wanders among his people incognito, that he may discover how they regard him. He finds no true loyalty, even personal affection evades him; his court and his family are enraged by his reforms the other crowned heads of Europe, the members of his social family, disdain him, and the very people, for whom he makes these sacrifices, look upon him with suspicion. At last, among the courtiers who have protested most, he seeks for a genuine devotion to his person; he is rewarded merely by phrases, and, in a paroxysm of despair, like the Hedda Gabler of fifteen years later, he shoots himself to escape from a world where he is in everybody's way.

As the working out of a startling psychological problem *The King* is worthy of very high praise. The extraordinary interest of the drama lies in this, that we share the internal agony of the solitary monarch, and follow him up the stages of his Calvary. An element of vain and melancholy love is introduced, greatly to the heightening of the pathos. Among all the imaginative works which the anomalous condition of royalty has called forth in late years, *The King* of Björnson is certainly the finest. The poet, unquestionably, produced it in good faith, as a reduction of the problem of constitutional government. It was not received as a very useful contribution to practical politics, and it involved the poet in every species of annoyance. In particular, the drama was taken as a personal attack upon the existing King of Sweden and Norway, who, like the hero of the piece, was a poet and had been a sailor. These resemblances were certainly accidental, but Björnson consented to modify them, and explained his position in a dignified apology. The poem had been composed at Aulestad, in the midst of a republican agitation that will account for the temper of it.

Two years later, in April 1879, the drama called *Leonarda* was produced on the stage of the Christiania Theatre ; in September of the same year, the book was published in Copenhagen. In the latter city, its performance was successfully opposed by the censor, Christian Molbech, and a violent controversy resulted. It was only natural that a drama, the central idea of which was to inculcate toleration in religious and in social matters should be intolerantly opposed by all in positions of conventional responsibility. But this time Björnson had not the pain of seeing any division formed among his poetical admirers. In *Leonarda* criticism was unanimous in discovering an ample stroke, a breadth and splendour in the depicting of passion, a truly poignant skill in dealing with the problems of the heart. *Leonarda* is a creation of extraordinary beauty ; it is my personal conviction that Björnson has never surpassed and has rarely elsewhere approached the beauty of many of its scenes.

The psychological action of the drama centres around Madame Leonarda Falk, a woman of business, the head of a firm in one of the principal Norwegian cities. Her earlier life is the subject of much speculation, and so little is known of it that the neighbourhood does not visit her, in spite of her wealth, her beauty, and her wit. She has no children, but has adopted a niece, Aagaat, to whom she is devoted. To the vague scandal of her early life, however, Leonarda adds the heinous offence of never coming to church, and her niece is included with herself in tbe social ban. One of the local clerics falls in love with Aagaat, and afterwards still more seriously with Leonarda herself; the intrigue of the play is engaged with the action of Leonarda in this new combination of circumstances.

One of the chief secondary charms of the play is the character of a bishop's aged grandmother, who retains the elaborate manners and elegant tolerance of the freethinkers of the last century, with whom her youth was passed, and still clings to a library which the rest of her family thinks exceedingly objectionable. This old lady regards with antipathy and disgust the fanaticism which has become the rule in the society around her, and welcomes a fresh opportunity for tolerance. When she hears of Leonarda's resolution, she exclaims, "Then the age of great emotions has come back again," and this is the key-note of the play. It is a jovial protest against the conventionality and formal respectability of the age, and a heralding of a wholesomer time at hand.

Six weeks after the publication of *Leonarda*, Björnson produced a drama called *The New System* ("Det Ny System"). This is a comedy of manners, written not without ingenuity, but on the whole of inferior importance.

To understand the position of Björnson, it is necessary to remember that Ibsen had at length come to entertain precisely similar views with regard to the form of social drama. In 1877 he had produced *The Pillars of Society*, a play in some respects more severely realistic than anything which Björnson had written. In *The New System* we find Björnson turning to compete with this dangerous rival. He has purged his style of all its fantastic and lyrical elements, and tries to be as stern a naturalist as Ibsen. When Maupassant wrote *Nôtre Cœur*, he was attempting to show that he could perform the Bourget trick as well as Bourget himself; in *The New System*, in the same way, Björnson is assuring his readers that he understands every secret of the art of Ibsen. Even the plot is dangerously similar to that of *The Pillars of Society.* Mr. Riis, the rich director of a company, has a " new system " of conducting business (we are not clearly informed of its character, but it is fraudulent, and it costs the country millions) which has raised his family into affluence. A young engineer, who is the son of an old disreputable friend to whom Riis has always been kind, finds it his duty to expose " the new system "; but he is in love with Riis' daughter. Conscience struggles with passion through five acts, but at last he performs his act of exposure, and everybody deserts Riis except his wife. There is a good deal of sparkling social writing and some pathos in *The New System,* but it is pale by the side of the Ibsen dramas which it was intended to compete with, and it was promptly extinguished in the excitement caused a few weeks later by the publication of *A Doll's House.*

In the disappointment which followed, Björnson was long time silent as a dramatist. His great rival brought out *Ghosts* and then *The Enemy of the People.* The moral force of these bitter satires was not lost on Björnson, who, when once more he appeared before the footlights, came forward, he also in the popular capacity of a moral reformer. *A Gauntlet* ("En Hanske") was published in the autumn of 1883, but once more the Norwegian poet had the vexation to see the theatres of Scandinavia closed to its representation. Although his dramas are not more violent or startling, Björnson has been much less lucky than Ibsen in getting them promptly put on the stage in his own country; he has commonly had to be content with performances at Hamburg, Berlin or Vienna, while Ibsen has never been unable to produce one of his social dramas in the leading theatres of the three Scandinavian capitals within a few weeks of publication.

In *A Gauntlet*, Björnson deals, paradoxically and flightily, but with considerable courage and freshness, with one of those problems in which Alexandre Dumas *fils* delights. Svava Riis, an enthusiastic girl of the upper middle class, is betrothed to a young man of eligible social character. The arrangement has originally been one of *convenance*, but Alf Christensen has grown to love Svava with all his heart. Just before the wedding, however, the past life of her *fiancé* is brought to Svava's knowledge, and the purity of her virginal conscience is so revolted that, in the very midst of the wedding festivities, she metaphorically flings her glove in his face, and refuses to marry him. This play produced in Scandinavia something of the same excitement as did *The Heavenly Twins* with us a decade later. It had passages of delicious humour, which relieved the strained emotion of the central idea. Nothing could be funnier than the scene in which the father and mother of the intended bridegroom call upon the parents of the bride, and discuss the unfortunate shortcomings of the young man in discreet Pecksniffian language, not shocked at all, but a little embarrassed, at the discovery of this " past " and these inconvenient wild oats.

In writing *A Gauntlet*, Björnson attained for the first time a complete skill in awakening that " emotional curiosity " which has been described as the most prominent aim of his later dramas. He had nowhere before been so eminently modern, so completely in sympathy with those who in our generation analyse and determine all the vague and ambiguous sensations which govern our moral actions. His psychology had now become delicate and penetrating, although the general results of his investigation were, as they still are, troubled by his desire to preach, by his instinct as an agitator and a revolutionist. In this he has always been curiously distinguished from Ibsen, who does not desire to teach anything, who has no "lesson" to convey, but who pursues his clinical examination of the social patient with the severity of a hospital surgeon. Björnson, of a temperament tenderer and far less calm, is not content to diagnose the disease; he wishes to cure it also. This double aim, this tendency to combine art with propaganda, disturbs the conduct of his plays and renders their form imperfect. It is none the less undeniable that it adds to them the charm of a very lovable humanity.

Since the theatres of his country would not present his plays to the public, Björnson grew more and more indifferent to the actable character of them, and in *Over Ævne* (a title almost impossible to translate, but of which the words "Out of Reach," give some idea) he published a dramatic poem in prose without thought of the practical stage. In accordance with the author's partiality for bringing out his productions in pairs, it appeared six weeks after *A Gauntlet*, in the autumn of 1883. *Over Ævne* is a dramatic fragment in two acts, dealing with the phenomena of religious hysteria and hallucination. The scene is laid far up in the Arctic part of Norway, on the coast where the roar of the Atlantic is never still, breaking at the foot of strange, melancholy mountains "that are like no other mountains." Here Pastor Sang lives the life of a missionary martyr, and by dint of vehement prayer, he comes to work miracles ; he seems, at least, to have raised an old bed-ridden woman, to have cured a dying child. His own wife falls ill of a slow wasting disease ; Sang goes to the church, and will wrestle there with God until she recovers. Meanwhile the Bishop arrives, with his suite of clerics, drawn by the rumour of marvellous events. Klara Sang rises from her bed, cured ; the pastor praying in the church, is conscious of her recovery. They turn to meet, but at the church door each falls dead in the arms of the other.

In *Over Ævne* all is fantastic, symbolical, miraculous. It is a study in hystero-epilepsy, if you will, but of the spiritual conditions much more than the physical. The sense of over-strained religious excitement moving within a very small circle in the midst of abnormal physical conditions is given with so much gusto that the author seems a fellow-believer more than an observer. In no work of modern drama does landscape take a larger place : although they are scarcely mentioned, we are conscious throughout of the cliffs, the dark ice-cold fjord, the dolphin colours of the midnight sky where the sun wheels round, but never sets. The promised " second part " of *Over Ævne*, the author has never given us. The little volume of 1883 remains a profoundly suggestive and poetical, but puzzling and even incoherent fragment, an attempt to turn the theories of Charcot and Krafft-Ebing into drama by a writer of genius who did not wholly understand them.

One more play has to be mentioned in dealing with this section of Björnson's work, the comedy of *Geography and Love* (" Geographi og Kærlighed "), 1889. In this the influence of Ibsen is strongly apparent, so strongly that the native manner of Björnson seems disturbed by it. In this curious piece, a learned and highly successful Norwegian writer on geography is shown to be so completely absorbed in his investigations, that he sacrifices the comfort of his domestic circle to them. His daughter is sent off to a boarding-school, that her room may be used for maps and charts, while his notes, in little heaps, each with a small stone to weigh it down, more and more invade the living rooms and his wife's personal domains. As a study of the nervous egotism and unbridled temper of a highly-strung pedant, the first act is admirable ; Björnson has done no better scenes of comedy than those in which the women-folk of the geographer rise up at last in revolt against their tyrant, and fly for their lives from his Blue-beard castle. In the second act he is alone, delighted at first with his freedom and solitude, then terribly bored and alarmed at the absence of all the petting he is used to. The third and final act is, to my thinking, preposterous. It is all Mæterlinck and psychical research. The geographer is in Bessarabia, but he is also, in astral form, at home in Christiania, and he haunts his own drawing-room and wine-cellar. All this is very bewildering and tortured, the action sinking to a sort of mad spectral frolic, or tragical farce. It is a pity that *Geography and Love* should end so crazily, for the beginning of it is exceedingly alert and entertaining ; and in the reunion of husband and wife, just before the curtain falls, we have a touch of delicate humanity.

The social dramas of Björnson have been described here with some fulness, because they form a very important section of his work, and one which is little known in this country. It is imperative to compare them with those of Ibsen, because they really resemble no other literary products of the age, and the two series are closely allied to one another. It may be said that the differences between them, though considerable, are specific, their inter-relation generic and essential. The distinction is that Björnson seems to have less to say and less force in saying it than Ibsen, but possesses a lighter, gayer touch, more variety and a sweeter temper. They are to one another as Decker to Cyril Tourneur among our old playwrights, or as Alphonse Daudet to Zola. The younger dramatist is the less impersonal. In reading *Ghosts* or *Hedda Gabler* we do not think of the writer ; in reading *The King* or *A Gauntlet* we enjoy the sense of Björnson's individuality. The latter plays combine to a high degree observation and fancy ; reality is used in them to heighten the sentiments of wonder and curiosity. The two modes are constantly interacting, and if there is something of Ibsen in *Geography and Love*, there is undoubtedly a great deal of Björnson in *The Master-Builder*. Finally, if Björnson is occasionally more brilliant in the conduct of a single scene, Ibsen is almost always more successful in the architecture of an entire play.

VII

We now approach a period in Björnson's literary life where it is difficult and even dangerous for criticism to follow him. During the last ten years his appearances have been few, and with a single exception they have been confined to fiction. After a long retirement from the novel, he returned to it in 1884 with the remarkable volume entitled *Det Flager i Byen og paa Havnen* ("Flags are Flying in Town and Port"), the longest book, indeed the only book *de longue haleine*, which he had published in his busy life. Five years later, in 1889, he produced another as lengthy and still more remarkable novel, *Paa Guds Veje* ("In God's Way"). During the same decade, several short stories, of a more or less vivid nature—*Stöv* ("Dust") is doubtless the most striking of them—have appeared from his pen, and as I write, in August 1894, there arrives from Copenhagen a volume of *Nye Fortællinger* ("New Stories"), a group of four tales, one of which, at least, *Mors Hænder* ("Mother's Hands"), is certainly not quite new. In this collection, the opening story, *Absaloms Haar* ("Absalom's Hair"), is the most remarkable. These, then, are the elements on which a judgment of the latest Björnson have to be based, and I confess that it is not easy to retire far enough back from them to obtain the requisite aërial perspective.

The two long novels which have just been named are the works by which Björnson is best known to the present generation of Englishmen. They possess elements which have proved

excessively attractive to certain sections of our
public ; indeed, in the case of *In God's Way*, a
novel, which was by no means successful in its
own country at its original publication, has
enjoyed an aftermath of popularity in Scandinavia, founded on reflected warmth from its
English admirers. It cannot but be admitted that
these are interesting books, original and pleasing
in their evolution, well executed in detail and
full of valuable and exact observation of human
life.   In each, the growth of character is chroni-
cled with so agreeable a fidelity to nature, that
the attention is riveted until the narrative is—
not completed, for Björnson never completes—but
relinquished.   In these two novels, moreover,
Björnson returns, in measure, to the poetical
elements of his youth.   He is now capable
again, as for instance in the episode of Ragni's
symbolical walk in the woodlands, in *In God's
Way*, of passages of a pure idealism.   The
character of Ragni, throughout, in relation to
scenery and physical phenomena, is sustained at
a high imaginative level.   If we judged by these
two books alone, we should conceive that Björnson had lost his worst provincial faults, had
gained firmness and consistency of treatment,
and was on his road to successes greater than
any that he had yet dreamed of.

His shorter stories, advanced as they are with at least as much complacency, force us to pause and question. If we take the very latest of them, *Absalom's Hair*, we are perplexed and disconcerted by the evidence which it presents to us of confusion in the mind of its author. So, we say to ourselves, a very young man of extraordinary talent may pour forth his volcanic ideas, without selection, without arrangement ; but that a veteran of sixty-two summers, busied on the art of composition from his boyhood up, should be content with such manifestations of talent, this is embarrassing indeed. We have before us constantly the allegory or symbol of Absalom's hair, of the long tresses which capture the revolting son while he pursues his venerable and outraged father, and we no less constantly compare with it the narrative of Rafael Kaas, which it is supposed to illustrate, but which really gains from it no more illumination than a figure in a dark room obtains from a candle passed across behind it. The links are wanting which are needed to show us where the fate of Rafael resembled that of Absalom. It is impossible to doubt that the poet selected the symbol before he had worked out the story, that the character of his hero led him whither he would not, and that whenever we meet with a startling reminiscence of Absalom, it is the result of a sudden recollection on Björnson's part that he has already selected a name for the narrative.

Great seems to be the divergence from the path indicated in *Synnöve Solbakken* to that pursued in the *Fortællinger* of to-day. But it may well be that the dimness of vision is ours, and that a later criticism may see a consistent evolution running through Björnson's writings. We can perceive already that, although affected by many conflicting influences, he has remained throughout essentially himself. He was subjected at first to the forces of German romanticism, then, through Oehlenschläger, to Victor Hugo, and then to French naturalism ; he bowed to each in turn, but each passed away and left him unbent. He has striven hard to be a realist, and at times he has seemed to acquiesce altogether in the naturalistic formula, but in truth he has never had anything essential in common with M. Zola.

Björnson is practically the best living instance of what M. Edouard Rod calls "intuitivism" in imaginative literature. He does not argue or generalise; he forms, without reasoning, a perception of character, and he puts this perception on paper, with agitation, with a certain precipitancy of the sensitive conscious-

ness, convinced that disturbance will destroy for
ever the fugitive idea. Hence the occasional
incongruity of his forms; hence the almost
constant inability to tie up the ends of a story,
to conduct it to a harmonious and graceful close.
The intuition ceases, and with it the tale must
cease. The author is actuated by no series of
principles, is attended by no array of collected
phenomena, but is a free lance dependent
entirely on the dash and impetus of his immediate apprehension. If this distinction be seized
and accepted, it is seen to place a chasm, not
merely between the Naturalists and Björnson,
but between him and such writers as Tolstoi and
Dostoieffsky.

If this be true, and I believe that in no other
way can the oddities of Björnson's attitude
towards life and literature be explained, it leads
us to a certain regret that he should not have
resigned himself more frankly than he has done
to his singular gift of instinctive appreciation.
With such flashing insight, with so little need
to lean upon experimental knowledge, he should
have been pre-eminently an artist. But his
whole effort seems to have been to quench the
artist in himself, and to urge into activity a
prophet, a hieratic personage, whom he conceived to be devoted to sacred uses and the

renovation of mankind. Not without danger, not without a dimming of the vision and a troubling of the waters, can an intuitivist of the Björnson order resolutely turn his attention away from all the aspects of life save those which surround the bases of our social and of our moral being. Björnson was born into the world a fighter. He is not content to contemplate or to create ; he must be pulling down and digging up. For him, the pessimistic attitude of Ibsen—so cold, so dignified, so self-restrained—presumes an intolerable bondage. Björnson would die in such an atmosphere, like an eagle in a Leyden jar ; he longs to act, to correct, to ameliorate social conditions. All this at once animates and weakens his literary production. Ceaseless revolt is not a favourable attitude for poetical composition, nor is mere temerity in itself an illumination, and Björnson would, in this year of grace, be a more charming writer, if he had gradually allowed the turbulent vehemence of his youth to evaporate, instead of carefully generating and feeding it.

Such restrictions, however, lack wisdom no less than they lack grace, since, after all, what a persistent charm this vivid Norwegian writer preserves, what an odour of youth, what a breeze of delicious vitality ! Björnson's belief in the future of the race is robust and cheering. We feel that, like the pilgrim of Asolo, he is

One who never turned his back but marched breast forward,
  Never doubted clouds would break,
Never dreamed, though right were worsted, wrong would
    triumph,
Held we fall to rise, are baffled to fight better,
                                          Sleep to wake.

Now Browning has left us, Björnson is the one great optimist left in Europe, and his cheery confidence covers a thousand irregularities of temperament. It brings him at once into harmony with the public, which is not keen to perceive small inconsistencies nor to apprehend nice definitions of style, but which recognises and warmly welcomes a writer that loves it, and that speaks straight to its heart.

In his long and various career as a writer, throughout the vicissitudes which have led him from *Synnöve Solbakken* to *Absalom's Hair*, in the midst of much bewilderment and confusion, and a tangled web of designs, Björnson has held tightly to one or two fortunate strands which his genius placed in his new-born fingers. One of these is an impassioned love of his country, spoiled by no cynicism or false shame, and extending, through its people, to the phenomena of its meadows and its mountains ; another is a happy intuitive insight into the

hearts of women, and a singular skill in following their secret meditations. These are idyllic
qualities, and we come back to the conclusion
that Björnson—agitator, warrior, shouter as he
is in the windy trenches—was pre-eminently
intended by nature to be an idyllist. *Rusticus es,
Corydon;* and it is Björnson's most distinguishing
merit that, with an enchanting freshness, he was
the first to reveal to us the exquisite characteristics of the peasantry of his native country.

EDMUND GOSSE.

BIBLIOGRAPHICAL NOTE

[SYNNÖVÉ SOLBAKKEN *appeared in September 1857 as a holiday number of a popular illustrated newspaper which Björnson was editing in Christiania. It attracted attention at once, and the edition was sold out before the close of the year. A second issue, in handsomer form, printed in Copenhagen, but still published in Christiania, appeared in January 1858. There were six separate editions before, in 1872, it was included in the collected* Fortællinger, *in which form it has since appeared. It was translated into German in 1859, and frequently since; into Dutch in the same year, into Spanish in 1865, into French in 1868, into Russian in 1869, and into English for the first time in 1870. The book was written in Copenhagen during the spring of 1857.*

E. G.]

SYNNÖVÉ SOLBAKKEN

SYNNÖVE SOLBAKKEN

CHAPTER I

AMID the Norwegian valleys there are favoured spots of lowlands rising into gentle eminence, lying open to the sunlight from the first of the ruddy dawn to the last beam gilding the west. People who live more in the shadow of the hills, having less of the sun, call such a spot a " sunnyside."* She of whom this story tells lived on such a sunnyside, from which the farm also took its name. There the snow covered the ground latest in the autumn, and melted away sooner than elsewhere in the spring.

The owners of the farm were Haugists,† the people called them " readers," because they read

---

* Solbakke.

† So called after Hauge (1771-1824), the founder of a religious sect.

the Bible more diligently than their neighbours.
The man's name was Guttorm, the wife's Karen.
They had a boy, but he died, and for three years
they shunned that part of the church where the
font stood. Then they had a little girl, whom
they called after the boy. His name had been
Syvert, and she was christened Synnöv, this
being the nearest in sound they could think of.
But the mother changed it to Synnövé, because
she used to say to the baby, Synnövé mine, and
she thought this was easier than Synnöv mine.
However that may be, the girl grew up to be
called Synnövé by everybody who knew her ; and
people said that in the memory of men there
had not been a lovelier girl in the valley than
Synnövé Solbakken.

She was very small when the parents began
to take her with them to church on preaching-
Sundays, although the little thing scarcely understood more than that the Pastor seemed to be
scolding down upon Jail-Ben, as people called
him, because he had been to prison once, and who
now sat just beneath the pulpit. But the father
wished the child to go that she might " get used
to going," and the mother wished it too, for " one

could not tell what might happen to her at home."
If any creature on the farm, a lamb, or a kid, or
a sucking-pig, would not thrive, or if a cow ailed,
it was made over to Synnöve, and called her
property; and the mother declared that the
animals were sure to do well from that moment.
The father did not quite believe in the remedy,
but "it did not matter which of them owned the
beasts, provided that they throve."

On the opposite side of the valley, and close
to the foot of the mountain, lay the farm
Granliden,* so called because it was surrounded
by a forest of fir-trees, the only fir wood far and
wide. The great-grandfather of the present
owner had been with a regiment, quartered in
Holstein, to fight the Russians; and from that
country he had brought back in his knapsack
a quantity of foreign seeds. These he sowed
all round the farm, but in course of time the
plants died off; a few fir cones, however,
which had chanced to be among his treasures,
took root, grew and multiplied, spreading into
a forest which now on all sides overshadowed
the farm.

* Fir side.

The man who had been to Holstein was called after his grandfather Thorbjörn ; his own eldest son he called after his father Sämund; in fact, the owners of this farm, as far back as memory would reach, had always been Thorbjörns and Sämunds in turn. But people said that at Granliden only every other owner was happy, and that was not he who bore the name of Thorbjörn. When the present owner, Sämund, came to christen his eldest boy he considered long ; but after all he did not quite like to break with the time-honoured family custom, and the boy was called Thorbjörn. Then he considered whether the boy could not be so brought up that he might be saved from the trouble which tradition and the talk of the people seemed to make sure of for him. Of this he did not feel certain, but he thought to observe an unruly spirit in the boy. "This must be thrashed out of him," said he to the mother ; and when Thorbjörn was barely three years old, the father made a point of sitting down, birch-rod in hand, making the boy carry back to its place every log of wood he had flung about, or forcing him to stroke the cat which he had pinched. But the

4

mother would leave the room when the father was in one of these moods.

Sämund used to wonder why the boy needed more and more correction the older he grew, and this in spite of the great severity with which he brought him up. Very early the father made him take to his spelling-book, and then took him about on the farm with him, that he might have an eye to his doings. The mother had a large household to look after, and small babies besides; she could do no more than kiss the child and give him good admonition when she helped him to dress in the morning, and speak lovingly to the father when they all sat together on Sundays or other times of rest. But when Thorbjörn was beaten because *a b* did not spell *ba*, but *ab*, or when he was not allowed to thrash little Ingrid as the father thrashed him, he used to think within himself: " Why *should* I have all the blows, when my little brothers and sisters get none ! "

As he generally went about with the father, and rather stood in awe of him, he spoke little, but not because he thought little. Once, however, when they were busy drying the hay, he ventured the question :

"Why is it that at Solbakken the hay is always in long before ours?"

"Because they have more sun than we."

Then for the first time the thought struck him that he himself was outside the sunshine which seemed to be over there, and which he had liked to watch ever since he could remember. And from that day he gazed at Solbakken even oftener than before.

"What are you staring at?" said the father, and gave him a push. "We must work down here, young and old, if we are to get along."

When Thorbjörn was about seven or eight years old, his father engaged a new farm lad, whose name was Aslak, and who had been about the world a good deal already, although he was but a boy. When he arrived it was evening, and the children were in bed; but the following morning, when Thorbjörn sat at his lessons, somebody flung the door open with such a noise as he had never heard before. It was Aslak coming in with a big armful of firewood, which he threw down so as to send the logs flying in all directions over the floor, himself stamping and jumping to shake off the snow, shouting as he did so :

" It is cold, said the bride of the goblin ; and the ice covered her to the chin."

The father was not at home, but the mother swept the snow together and carried it out, saying nothing.

" And what *are* you looking at ? " demanded Aslak of Thorbjörn.

" Nothing," said the little boy, for he was afraid.

" Have you seen the cock at the end of your book ? "

" Yes."

" He has a lot of hens about him when the book is closed—have you seen *that ?* "

" No."

" Then look ! "

The little boy looked.

" You silly donkey," said Aslak.

But from that day no one had such power over him as Aslak.

" You know nothing at all," said Aslak one day to Thorbjörn, who, as usual, was following him about to see what he was doing.

"Yes, I do ; I can say the Catechism almost through."

"Rubbish! you don't even know the story of the goblin who danced with the girl till the sun went down, and then burst like a calf that has drunk butter-milk."

Never in his life had Thorbjörn heard such learning.

"Where was it ? " he asked.

"Where ?——oh, let me see——why, yes, it was over there at Solbakken."

Thorbjörn stared.

"And I suppose you never heard of the man who sold his soul to the devil for a pair of old boots ? "

Thorbjörn, amazed, could not answer.

"I daresay you would like to know where *that* was—wouldn't you ?——That, too, happened at Solbakken, just there, close by the brook which you can see.——Bless me ! " he continued after a while, "your education has been most dreadfully neglected ! I suppose you never heard of the Kari who wore a wooden petticoat ? "

No ; he had never heard of her.

And Aslak, working away merrily, talked away more merrily still—wonderful stories of Kari who wore the wooden petticoat ; of the mill which ground the salt at the bottom of the sea ; of the goblin who was caught by the beard in an alder·tree ; of the seven green damsels pulling the hairs out of Lazy John's calves, who wanted to wake up but could not ;—and all these things had actually happened at Solbakken.

"What on earth has come over the boy ? " said the mother the following day, which chanced to be Sunday ; " since the early morning he has not moved from the window, staring away at Solbakken."

"Yes, he seems wonderfully taken up," said the father, stretching himself as he enjoyed the day of rest.

"People say he is engaged to be married to Synnöve Solbakken," remarked Aslak quietly ; " but people *do* talk ! "

Thorbjörn did not quite know what he meant, yet he grew red all over the face.

And as Aslak jeered at this, he crept down from the window, took his Catechism, and began to learn assiduously.

" That's right ! " said Aslak, "console yourself with the Christian's duty, for you'll never
get her."

As the week advanced, Thorbjörn thought the
matter might be forgotten. And he asked his
mother—rather softly, for he felt as though he
ought to be ashamed:

" Mother, who is Synnövé Solbakken ? "

" That's a little girl who one day will become
the mistress of Solbakken."

" Does she wear a wooden petticoat ? "

The mother opened her eyes.

" Wear *what?* " she asked.

He thought he must have said something silly,
and did not repeat it.

" There has never been a more beautiful child
than Synnövé," continued the mother ; " and no
doubt God made her so because she is always
good and obedient and mindful of her lessons."

Well, that too was information.

One day when Sämund had been working on
the farm with Aslak, he said to Thorbjörn in the
evening :

" I won't have you holding any more inter-
course with that boy."

But Thorbjörn did not seem to remember the injunction. A few days later the command was therefore strengthened :

" If I see you again with him you'll catch it ! "

And then Thorbjörn grew cautious, and only talked with Aslak when he thought the father did not see. But the father did see—Thorbjörn had a whipping, and was sent indoors. After this he tried to meet Aslak only when he knew the father to be from home.

One Sunday, when the father had gone to church, Thorbjörn enjoyed what he considered his liberty at home. He and Aslak pelted each other with snowballs.

" Please, you are hurting me," said Thorbjörn after some play ; " let's throw them at something else."

Aslak was agreeable ; they sent the balls flying, first towards a small fir-tree which grew by the storehouse, then towards the door, and at last towards the window of the storeroom.

" Not the window itself," explained Aslak, " only against the framework."

But Thorbjörn caught a pane and looked terrified.

"Stupid! who'll know it?" said Aslak; "take better aim."

Thorbjörn sent another ball—a second time cracking the glass.

"Now I shall stop," he said.

At this moment his sister next in age, little Ingrid, came from the house.

"Throw it at *her!*"

Thorbjörn took the hint; the girl began to cry, which brought the mother to the scene. She forbade the snowballing.

"Throw it! throw it!" said Aslak under his breath.

Thorbjörn's blood was up—he threw the ball.

"Are you beside yourself, boy?" exclaimed the mother, turning on him; but he ran away, and she after him round the house. Aslak looked on, grinning. At last the mother caught Thorbjörn on a snow heap, intending to punish him.

"If you strike—I'll strike back—that I will!"

The mother's hand dropped; she stood aghast.

"This is the other's teaching," she said—took him by the hand quietly, and drew him after her within doors. Not a word further did she address to him, but as she occupied herself with his little brothers and sisters he heard her say that now the father would soon be coming home from church. The room grew hotter and hotter till it felt stifling. Aslak asked leave to go and see an acquaintance of his; permission was at once given. Thorbjörn's spirit sank more and more; it seemed an awful look-out, an agony of terror eating away at his heart. All around him appeared to know what was coming; the very clock kept on saying: " Catch—blows, catch—blows ! " and no help for it. He climbed the window-sill and looked over to Solbakken. There it was, lonely and restful, covered with snow, yet ever beaming in the sunlight, which glowed and glowed till every window wore a smile—no panes could have been broken there ! How boldly the smoke ascended from the chimney; they, too, would be getting dinner ready for those who had gone to church. And Synnöve ?—she also would be looking for her father, but surely no blows were in store for her when he came home. He did not know what to do with himself; but he grew tenderly demonstrative towards his little sisters. Towards Ingrid especially he felt so moved that he presented her with a bright brass button which Aslak had given him. She kissed him for it, and he put his arms round her.

" Dear little Ingrid, are you angry with me ? "

" No, Thorbjörn, dear ! And you may throw as many snowballs at me as you like."

There was a noise outside the door, somebody stamping about to get clear of the snow. The door opened—it was the father ! He looked mild, and most benevolent, which seemed worse than a frown.

" Well ? " he said, looking about ; and Thorbjörn would not have thought it strange to see the tell-tale clock come down bodily from the wall.

The mother put his dinner on the table.

" Well ! and how have things been going on here ? " asked the father, possessing himself of a spoon.

Thorbjörn looked at the mother, and saw her double in his rising tears.

" Oh—very well," she answered slowly ; yes, she was going to say more, he knew it. " I gave Aslak permission to go out," she added quietly.

" Now it is coming," thought Thorbjörn, and began to play with Ingrid with an earnestness as if there were nothing in the world besides.

The father had never been such a time over his dinner! At last Thorbjörn began to count his mouthfuls, and then he tried how much he could count between the fourth and fifth mouthful, which brought his figures to a muddle, and he gave it up. The father rose and went out. "The panes—the panes," the clock was saying, He looked if those in the room were all right. Yes—none were broken there. But now the mother, too, left the room. Thorbjörn took little Ingrid on his knees, and said to her so gently that she looked at him astonished :

" Shall we play ' Gold-King of the Meadow '— shall we, dear ? "

Yes, she would like it ; and he sang, his knees knocking together with anguish :

> " Little flower, meadow-sweet,
> Listen to my say :

15

If thou wilt be my little bride
I'll give myself and more beside:
A cloak of gold,
And it shall hold
A pearl untold.
Ditteli, dutteli, di—
The sun shines well on high!"

To which the little girl made answer:

" Gold-King of the meadow,
Listen to my say:
I will not be thy little bride,
And do not want thy gifts beside :
No cloak of gold
That could infold
A pearl untold.
Ditteli, dutteli, di—
The sun shines well on high!"

But just as they were in the best of their play
the father re-entered the room, looking hard at
Thorbjörn. He caught Ingrid tighter in his
arms, and actually did not fall from his chair.
The father turned away without saying a word.
Half an hour went by, and yet he had said
nothing. Thorbjörn almost began to feel well
again—if only he dared. Yet when the evening
came, and the father himself helped to undress
the boy, his heart again misgave him. What was
this ? the father patting his head, and stroking

his cheeks! He had not done this as long as the boy could remember. He felt a warmth stealing about his heart, and throughout his body, which made his fears melt away as ice when the sun is shining. He hardly knew how he got into bed; and as he could neither sing nor scream for joy, he folded his hands quietly over his heart, and repeated very softly the Lord's Prayer six times forwards and six times backwards, and thought, as he fell asleep, that after all on God's wide earth there was no one he loved better than his own dear father.

In the morning he woke with a terrible sensation, as though he wanted to scream but could not; surely now the thrashing was coming! Opening his eyes he was relieved to find that he had been dreaming; yet he discovered that punishment was at hand, not for him but for Aslak. Sämund marched up and down the room; Thorbjörn knew that sort of walking. The strong man—he was rather short, but well-built—looked from time to time towards Aslak, and there was no mistaking those looks. Aslak, pretending the greatest unconcern, sat astride on a cask with his hands in his trouser pockets,

and wearing a cap squashed down over his forehead, his dark hair appearing in knotty lumps
from under it. With his head bent to one
shoulder the wry mouth looked more crooked
than ever, and from his half-closed eyes he shot
sidelong glances at Sämund.

"Yes," he said at last, "this boy of yours
seems quite an idiot; but what is worse for the
present is that your horse is bewitched."

Sämund stopped short.

"You impertinent rascal," said he, with a
voice that resounded through the room, and he
resumed his walking. Aslak shut his eyes more
closely, and sat quiet for a while.

"The animal really *is* bewitched," and he
gave a squint at his master to watch the effect of
this further assertion.

"Bewitched in that wood, yes," said Sämund,
walking on. "It's your doing, and nobody
else's, you good-for-nothing rascal—no wonder
he will not go quietly there!"

Aslak mused a while.

"You may believe as you please! Faith
hurts no man's soul, but I doubt whether it will
cure the animal"—he pushed himself back on

the cask and covered his face, holding up one arm.

Sämund indeed was coming towards him, saying in a low but ominous tone :

" You are a miserable—— "

" Sämund ! " called a voice from the hearth. It was Ingeborg, his wife, coming up to calm him, quieting at the same time the baby that was crying with fear. The child yielded, and so did Sämund ; but clenching his fist, which was rather small for such a strong-built man, he thrust it under Aslak's nose, holding it there while he fixed him with a look that spoke his mind. Then he paced about again without taking his eye from the culprit. Aslak was pale ; yet he managed to grin towards Thorbjörn with one side of his face, while the other side, being turned towards Sämund, kept its rigid appearance.

" The good God give us patience," he said calmly, but holding up his arms as if warding off a blow.

Sämund stood before him ; and stamping the ground with a vehemence that sent Aslak flying from his seat, he called out with the full power of his lungs :

" Do not name Him, you —— ! "

Ingeborg with the baby in her arm had flown to her husband and touched him gently. He did not look at her, but his arm fell. She sat down again ; the husband betook himself to walking about ; no one spoke, till Aslak, feeling the pressure of silence, began afresh :

" *Him !* I should say there is plenty for Him to mend at Granliden."

" Sämund ! Sämund ! " entreated Ingeborg. But Sämund had already caught hold of Aslak, although he had put out a leg this time to intercept the blow. The fellow, caught up by the collar and held fast by the leg, was flung with such force against the closed door that the panel gave way, and he himself turning a somersault flew through the sudden aperture. The mother, Thorbjörn, indeed all the children screamed and begged mercy for him—the house was filled with groans and terror. But Sämund was after him ; without as much as thinking of opening what remained of the door, he shivered the yet standing fragments to pieces, and, bursting through, he caught up Aslak a second time, carried him through the hall into the yard, and holding him

up high, he flung him to the ground. Seeing
that just there the snow was piled high and soft,
and could not hurt the boy, he snatched him up
a third time and carried him, as a wolf might
carry a disabled dog, to a place more free of
snow, where again he knocked him down and
then put his knee on the boy's chest. There is
no saying how it might have ended, had not
Ingeborg with the baby thrown herself between
them. "Do not make us all unhappy!" she
cried.

Ingeborg was sitting again in the room;
Thorbjörn dressed himself, and the father walked
up and down silently, drinking a little water from
time to time: the trembling of his hands was
such, that he could not hold the cup without
spilling some of its contents. Aslak did not
return, and Ingeborg rose, as if to go after him.

"Stay here," said Sämund in a distant sort of
voice, and she stayed.

He went himself and did not return.
Thorbjörn took his book and learned with
all his might, without, however, understanding
a single sentence.

Presently the house seemed to have recovered

itself; but there remained a feeling of strange interruption. Thorbjörn, after some time, ventured forth, and the first sight meeting his view was Aslak in the courtyard heaping his modest goods and chattels upon a small sledge. The little sledge was Thorbjörn's property. The boy watched him dismayed; Aslak indeed presented a woeful spectacle. His face and part of his clothes ran with blood. He coughed and kept feeling his chest. Silently he viewed Thorbjörn, then he said vehemently: "Boy, your eyes are a plague to me!" after which he put himself astride on the sledge and slid down the sloping road. "You won't see your sledge again in a hurry," said he with a parting grin, and turning yet again he put out his tongue at Thorbjörn. This was Aslak's departure.

A few days after, the policeman made his appearance at Granliden; and then the father was off and on from home; the mother shed tears, and she, too, seemed to have business that called her away from the household.

"What is it all about, mother?" asked Thorbjörn.

"It is all that boy Aslak," she said, and sighed.

One day also, little Ingrid was overheard singing an extraordinary ditty, which ran thus :

> "O thou lovely world—ah me—
> How my heart is sick of thee !
> The daughter does nothing but dancing about,
> The son is as stupid as any lout ;
> The mother's cooking is wretchedly poor,
> The father himself is the laziest boor.
> The cat is the cleverest of the lot,
> She steals the cream from the churning-pot."

There followed of course an investigation as to how the child was possessed of this song. She had it from her brother. Then Thorbjörn in tribulation owned that it was of Aslak's teaching.

"If I hear the like again, either from you or your sister," said the father, "you'll find a thrashing for it."

But worse than this, poor little Ingrid presently began to swear about the house. Thorbjörn was called to answer for it. And the father thought of resolving the investigation at once into condign punishment. The boy, however, cried so piteously, and made such good promises, that blows, for this time, remained suspended.

But the following preaching-Sunday the father said :

" There will be no opportunity for mischief at home. The boy will come with me to church."

CHAPTER II

THE church holds a high place in the estimation of the peasant; he sees it standing apart, lonely and sanctified. The sacred rest of the God's acre speaks to him without, the sound of the living Word within. It is the only house in the valley which he has thought worthy of adornment; its very steeple to him looks higher than it really is. The sound of its bells goes forth to meet him as he wends his way along on preaching-Sunday; and as often as he hears the peal he takes off his cap with a silent bend, as though he meant a "Thanks for the last!"* There is an understanding between him and these bells, known to him only. As a child he remembers listening to their call, watching the church-goers

---

* Tak for sidst—a usual greeting among Norwegian peasants; its meaning is something like this: "I remember gratefully our last happy meeting."

down the valley. The father went, he himself
was as yet too small to go. Many a picture had
interwoven itself with those grand and solemn
sounds, as for hours they continued to echo from
rock to rock. Three things especially seemed
part and parcel of the ringing bells—himself in
Sunday clothes, all the women looking their
best, the very horses in bright polished harness.

And when at last the Sunday dawns, the bells
of which bear witness to his own happiness,
when, for the first time in his life, in new
clothes—brand new, and somewhat large (for he
will grow)—he walks to church beside his
father, then, indeed, he hears joy and glory in
their peal! Are they not the keepers of doors
to things unknown ? And as he goes home the
sounds float after him—his mind is confused
with all he has seen and heard ; the singing and
the preaching, the choir and the table within the
rails, the many people, and all they wore ;—the
parting sounds deepen the mingling impressions,
and the church which he henceforth bears in his
heart is to him a living fact.

As he grows older he must go to the mountain
pasture with the cattle. The dewy Sunday

morning finds him sitting on some rock watching the cattle feed beneath him, and far away; he is alone, and as the rich sound of the church bells is borne up to him, silencing for a while the merry tinkle from among his cows, he feels a longing at his heart. For with the calling bells there seem to rise from the valley happy, joyful, and inviting thoughts—thoughts of the friends one would meet at church, of the happiness in being there, and the still greater happiness of having been, of the good dinner awaiting the church folk at home; thoughts of parents, of brothers and sisters, and happy evenings on the meadows behind the house; they are natural thoughts, and the sturdy little heart rebels against his lot. Yet the boy remembers it is the church bells that are ringing. He tries to think of some few verses such as they would sing at church, and folding his hands, with a long gaze down the valley, he sings them, and says the prayer he has been taught; after which he jumps up, and is happy again, blowing into his lure * till it resounds from the mountains.

In those silent valleys the church speaks yet a

* A long wooden horn.

language of its own to every listener, according
as the eye that beholds it is young or old.
Much may rise up between the church and the
grown man, but nothing will rise above it.
Awe-awakening and perfect, it stands before the
young about to be received in confirmation; it
raises a finger as it were, half threatening, half
beckoning, to the young man leading the maiden
to the altar; strong and upright it towers amid
the cares of manhood; restful and tender it looks
upon the old man's finished toil. It is during
service that the little children are brought to the
font, and everybody knows that the congregation
is never so devoutly joining as during the christ-
ening of the babies.

It is, in fact, impossible to view a true picture
of Norwegian peasants, good or bad, without
ever and again seeing the church in the fore-
ground. This may seem monotonous; but such
monotony is not against them. Once for all,
this should be borne in mind, though not exactly
on account of the church-going now to be
described.

Thorbjörn was highly delighted that at last he
too might come to church: there were many

things to be seen. While yet without the building his eyes felt dazzled with a variety of colouring truly startling; within he was awed by the silence that hovered over the congregation even before the service began; he forgot he should bend his head, yet seeing everybody else bend low, he forthwith followed the example. Then the singing began, the whole congregation about him falling in with one accord; he felt almost frightened. He sat quiet, but jumped as from a trance when their pew was opened and some one stepped in. The singing having come to an end, the father held out his hand to the new-comer, and said: "How do you do at Solbakken?"

Thorbjörn looked up amazed. But keenly as he eyed the man, he could see nothing about him that appeared in the least like charms and sorcery. His was a pleasant countenance, with fair hair, blue eyes, and a high forehead. He smiled when spoken to, and said "Yes" to everything that Sämund said, without, however, in the least appearing as though he had nothing to say.

"There, you can see little Synnöve," and

taking Thorbjörn on his knees, the father directed his attention to one of the women pews opposite.

A little girl was kneeling on the seat, looking over the top of the pew. She was fairer even than the man—indeed, her hair was fairer than anybody's Thorbjörn had ever seen. She wore red flying ribbons on the little cap from under which her flaxen hair appeared, and she was now laughing at him so merrily that for a time he could see nothing but her shining white teeth. In one hand she held a nicely bound hymn-book, in the other a tidily-folded handkerchief of red and yellow silk, and she was amusing herself by flapping the two together. The more he looked, the more he himself laughed back to her, and like her he wanted now to be kneeling on the seat. Then she nodded to him; he looked at her steadily, then he too nodded. She smiled and nodded a second time; he nodded back, and again and again. She smiled, but did not nod any more, till after a while, when he had forgotten, she once more nodded to him.

" I, too, want to look over! " he heard a voice

behind him, feeling himself at the same time pulled down by the legs, so that he almost toppled over. It was a small, strong-fisted urchin who now took possession of the vacated place. He, too, had light though bristling hair, and a pug nose. No doubt Aslak had informed Thorbjörn how troublesome boys whom he might meet with at school or in church should be treated. Accordingly, Thorbjörn pinched the youth from behind, so that he all but screamed with pain ; but he managed to gulp it down, descended, and caught Thorbjörn's ears. Thorbjörn in his turn snatched at the other's yellow wig, and pulled him over. Not even now did he scream, but he bit his adversary's calf. Thorbjörn pulled it from him, and held the boy's head tight to the ground. At this moment a hand caught him by the collar, lifting him up like a puppy dog, and he found himself back on his father's knee.

" If we were not in church you'd have a thrashing," he whispered in the boy's ear, at the same time pressing his hand till his very toes ached with the pain.

Then he remembered Synnövé and glanced

across. She still looked at him, but with so horrified an expression that he began to suspect he had misbehaved himself; had he been very naughty? As soon as the little girl caught his look, she crept down from her seat and did not show herself again.

Now the verger appeared, and then the pastor; he watched them attentively, and listened quietly to the service. He still sat on his father's knee, and went on thinking, "Won't she be looking up again?" The little boy who had begun the fight sat on a stool at the other end of the pew; he would have risen, but every time he attempted it he received a grip in the back from an old man who was nodding in the corner, but kept waking up as often as the boy moved. "Won't she be looking up again?" thought Thorbjörn, and every red ribbon he saw reminded him of hers; and every picture in the old church seemed either to be her height or not much less. Ah! —there the little flaxen head appeared, but she turned away, looking most serious, having caught his face.

Again the verger and the pastor demanded the boy's attention, the bells began to ring, and he saw that the congregation rose to leave the church.

The father resumed speaking with the fair-haired man, and both walked to the opposite pew, where the women too were stirring. The first who left it was a woman of fair hair like the man, and smiling like him, yet with a faint shadow in her smile. She was small and pale, holding Synnöve by the hand. Thorbjörn tried to get near the little girl, but she hid herself behind her mother's dress.

"Leave me alone!" said she.

"This little fellow, I suppose, has not been to church before," began the pale woman, putting her hand on his head.

"No, and that is why he comes to blows with his neighbour as soon as he gets there," said Sämund.

Thorbjörn looked up, ashamed, first at her, then at Synnöve, whom he now fancied more unfriendly than before. They left the church together, the parents in conversation and Thorbjörn behind Synnöve, who, however, took refuge in the folds of her mother's dress every time the boy approached her. He did not see the other boy again. Before the church door the party remained standing, having evidently much to talk about. Thorbjörn several times caught the name "Aslak," and as it seemed to him very possible his own name might come up as well, he moved to a safe distance.

"You need not be hearing this," said the mother to Synnöve; "go and talk to the boy, my child!"

Synnöve turned away hesitatingly; but Thorbjörn came up to her, and the two stood looking at each other for several minutes, silently. At last the girl said:

" For shame!"

"Why do you say so?"

" For shame!" she repeated more emphatically.

"What have I done wrong?"

" You have been fighting in church—and that while the pastor was saying the prayer. It was a shame!"

" Yes, but that is now some time ago."

Perhaps she saw the force of this reasoning, for she said, apparently mollified:

"Are you the boy whose name is Thorbjörn Granliden?"

"Yes ; and are you the girl whose name is Synnövé Solbakken ? "

"Yes——I always heard you were such a good boy."

" No—*that* is not true ; for I am the worst of us all."

" Well—who ever !—— " exclaimed Synnövé, putting her little hands together in utter astonishment. " Mother, mother, he says—— "

" Be quiet, child ! " was the reply, stopping her half-way as she was running to her parents. So she returned, but her big blue eyes kept looking towards her mother.

" I always heard *you* were such a good little girl," said Thorbjörn.

" Well, sometimes, when I have been learning my lessons," she assented.

" Is it true that there are goblins and witches and all sorts of sprites over at your place ? " asked he, putting his arm akimbo and resting on one leg, exactly as he had learned it from Aslak.

"Mother, mother, just listen to him ! He says—— "

"Leave me alone, child, I cannot listen— do not interrupt me again, do you hear ? "

So she had to retire a second time.

" Is it not true that among your hills there is strange music every night ? "

" No ! "

" Have you never seen a goblin ? "

" No ! "

" Lord bless me——— "

" Hush ! you must not say so ! "

" Why not ?—there is no harm——— "

" Yes, yes," she said, " and if you are not a good boy, you will have to go to hell ! "

" Do you think so ? " said he humbly, but relieved ; he had expected her to say, " You will get a thrashing ; " but the father stood not alarmingly near.

" Who is the strongest in your house ? " he asked presently, pushing his cap on one side.

" Why—I never thought ! "

" With us it's the father. He is so strong that he even got the better of Aslak ; and, you may believe me, Aslak is just a giant."

" Is he ? "

" He once lifted up a horse, legs and all."

" A horse ! "

"It is quite true, quite true—he himself told me."

This of course seemed conclusive.

" Who is Aslak ? "

" Oh! a naughty boy ; very naughty. The father gave him a bigger thrashing than anybody ever had before ! "

" Then thrashing is the fashion with you ? "

" Yes, sometimes——is there no thrashing at Solbakken ? "

" Oh no ! "

" Then what *do* you do ? "

" Well, the mother does cooking and knitting and sewing; so does Karin, but not nearly so well, for she is lazy. Father and the men work on the farm—sometimes they are at home."

He found this report quite satisfactory.

" But in the evening," she continued, " we read and sing hymns, and so we do on Sundays."

" All together ? "

" Yes."

" Well, that must be stupid work ! "

" Stupid work ! Mother, do you hear—— "

But she remembered the mother was not to be interrupted, and came back of her own accord.

"I have a great many sheep," she said, turning again to the boy.

"Have you, indeed?"

"Yes, and three of them will be lambing in the spring; one of them, I am sure, will have two."

"So you have sheep of your own?"

"Yes, and cows and little pigs. Haven't you any?"

"No."

"Then come over to me, and you shall have a lamb. And you'll get more by-and-by."

"That would be nice!"

For a while they meditated in silence. Then he asked:

"Couldn't Ingrid too have a lamb?"

"Who is she?"

"Ingrid—why it's little Ingrid!"

She had never heard of her.

"Is she smaller than you?"

"I should think so!——about as tall as yourself."

"O, well, then you must bring her when you come."

Certainly he would.

" But if I give you a lamb, she must have a little pig."

This appeared a fair arrangement; and then they began to enumerate their mutual acquaintances, of which there were not many. The parents meanwhile had done and were preparing to go home. So they had to separate.

In the following night Thorbjörn's dreams were of Solbakken—it was full of white lambs, and a little fair-haired girl with red ribbons went about among them. Ingrid and he spoke of nothing but the intended visit, and they seemed to have so many lambs and pigs to care for that all their time was taken up. But they were surprised their visit should not be carried out at once.

" Perhaps, because the little thing has invited you ? " asked the mother ; " who ever heard the like ! "

" Well, let's wait tell next church-going Sunday," said Thorbjörn to Ingrid ; " perhaps then ! "

The Sunday came.

" I hear you have such habits of bragging and swearing and story-telling, that you may not come to see me till you are a much better boy," said Synnöve to him.

" Who said so ? " asked Thorbjörn, astonished.

" Mother," replied she.

Ingrid awaited his return impatiently ; he told her and his mother what he had heard.

" Now you see ! " said the latter ; but Ingrid was silent.

* * * * *

Several months passed before the two were allowed to go over to Solbakken. And then Synnöve came to see them at Granliden, after which the two went again to see her, and she them ; so it went on till childhood was left behind. Thorbjörn and Synnöve vied with one another at lessons ; they went to the same school, and the boy did so well that the pastor began to take notice of him. Ingrid did not get on so fast, although Thorbjörn and Synnöve helped her. But she and Synnöve became the most inseparable of companions, and people called them the little snowbirds, because they always flew out together, and were both so exceedingly fair.

At times Synnöve had reason to be angry

with Thorbjörn, for he was quarrelsome, and often in a scrape; but then Ingrid acted as peacemaker, till the two were friends again.

If Synnövé's mother, however, heard of any of his misdoings, he was forbidden to show himself at Solbakken for the week, and for the matter of that did not always dare to show himself when the week of penitence was over! As for Sämund, it was not well to tell him of anything—"He is terribly hard upon the boy," said the mother, and tried to have things kept from him.

As they grew up, each of them grew handsome in a different way. Synnövé was tall and slender, with flaxen hair, a lovely-complexioned face, and quiet blue eyes. She smiled when she spoke, and people said it was a blessing to get within the reach of her smile. Ingrid was shorter and more robust; her hair was even fairer than Synnövé's, she had a small round face and soft features. Thorbjörn grew to middle height, but was very handsome and of powerful build. He had dark hair, deep-blue eyes, marked features, and well-shaped limbs. When he was angry he would say he could read and write as well as the schoolmaster, and feared not a man in the valley—"the father excepted," he added to himself, but did not say so.

Thorbjörn wanted to be confirmed early, but the father would not have it.

"Till you are confirmed, you are but a schoolboy, and I can manage you better!" said the father.

And so it came about that he, Synnövé, and Ingrid went together to the pastor to be prepared for confirmation. Synnövé, too, had waited longer than is usual, and was already in her sixteenth year.

"You cannot learn too much before making your confession of faith in confirmation," said the mother, and kept her at school beyond the customary age, Father Guttorm agreeing with her.

And thus it was not surprising that lovers already began to present themselves: one was the son of a good family in the neighbourhood, and the other a rich peasant in the valley.

"This is too bad!" says the mother, "and the child not even confirmed!"

" Then we must have her confirmed," said the father.

But Synnövé herself knew nothing of these suitors.

The ladies at the parsonage were fond of Synnövé, and used to call her in when the religious instruction was over, while Ingrid and Thorbjörn remained outside with the others. "Why didn't you slip in with her ? " asked one of the youths ; " somebody will be getting her before your very nose ! " This prediction cost the fellow a black eye, but the boys thenceforth took a pleasure in chaffing Thorbjörn about Synnövé, and it was found that nothing sent him into such a towering rage as the bare mention of her name.

All this twitting and chaffing, however, resulted in a great fighting fray among the boys ; it was settled the battle should come off in the wood at some distance from the parsonage. The girls had walked on, so there was no one who could have separated the infuriated youths. The number against Thorbjörn grew till almost the whole class stood against him. He had to defend himself tooth and nail, and many a blow.

was given, the subsequent results of which told their own tale. It became known, also, what the blows had been about, and there was much talking in the valley.

On the following Sunday Thorbjörn would not go to church, and when the next instruction-day came round he pretended illness ; so Ingrid went by herself to the pastor's. When she returned he inquired whether Synnövé had said anything.

" Nothing," was the answer.

But he had to appear again, and he thought everybody was reading his face. The boys laughed at him, though covertly. Synnövé arrived only when the class was just beginning, and remained behind with the ladies much longer than usual. He expected a lecture from the pastor, but found out presently that the only two in the valley who knew nothing of the affair were just the pastor and his own father. So far, things went well ; but it cost him much cogitation as to how he might talk again to Synnövé herself ; for the first time he dared not ask Ingrid to make it up between them. Synnövé stayed behind in the parsonage ; he waited till the last of the class had gone, when he too had to leave. Ingrid had left among the first.

The next time he found that Synnövé had come before any of the others, and was walking with one of the ladies and a young gentleman in the garden. The lady dug up some flowers, which she gave to Synnövé, the young gentleman assisting in the operation, while Thorbjörn, with his comrades, looked on through the paling. Synnövé was told how the flowers were to be planted—the conversation being loud enough for the outsiders to understand every word—and Synnövé said she would try and plant them again in her own little garden at home.

"You will want some help," said the gentleman. Thorbjörn heard this, and remembered.

When Synnövé came out to the others there was a general attempt to be agreeable to her. She went at once to Ingrid, and begged her to come with her to the lawn on the other side, where they seated themselves: it was long since they had had a talk. Thorbjorn meanwhile remained behind, examining the beautiful foreign flowers which had been given to Synnövé.

On that day she left the parsonage directly with the others.

"Shall I carry the flowers for you?" asked Thorbjörn.

"You may," she said quite pleasantly, but did not look at him.

She took Ingrid by the hand, leaving him to follow with the flowers. Having arrived at the place where their roads separated, she took the basket which he had set down beside her, merely saying:

"Thank you, I can easily carry them home myself now," and left, having shaken hands with Ingrid.

He had all along intended to offer his help for the planting of the flowers; but she had turned away so quickly, that he had not got his words together before she was gone. He was sorry afterwards, and wished he had asked her.

"What have you been talking about?" he inquired of Ingrid.

"Nothing particular," she said.

When everybody had gone to bed, Thorbjörn rose again, dressing himself cautiously, and went out. It was a lovely evening, soft and still. The sky had veiled itself, but the thin blue-grey clouds were torn here and there, and it looked as if eyes were upon him from the deeper sky beyond.

No one was to be seen on the farm, nor indeed anywhere in the distance. The grass-hoppers were chirping all around him; a wild-fowl was calling and being answered by another, and yet another, till there was a singing and calling all over the meadows, till it seemed to him as though the creatures all had risen to join in his expedition. Yet nothing was to be·seen. The fir-wood was of a bluish colour, rising darker and darker along the mountain-side, look-ing like a sea of mist. The blackcock's clarion sounded afar, some lonely owl screeched a song to herself, while the waterfall played away at a melody as old as the rock whence it sprang, and which seemed all the louder now that everything had settled down to listen. Thorbjörn cast a look at Solbakken, and marched away. Leaving the usual track, he went straight across field and meadow, and soon found himself in the little garden which was Synnöve's own, lying just beneath the window of her garret-room. He stood and listened, but nothing stirred. Then he looked about for some gardening tools, and discovered a spade and rake, probably the girl's own. Part of a flower-bed had already been dug up, but only a very small piece was actually ready, and there two flowers had been planted —as if to see how they would look. " The poor thing got tired over her work—it needs a man's arm to do it really," said he to himself, setting forthwith about his task. He felt wide awake, and never before had work appeared so easy. He remembered quite well how the flowers should be planted ; he remembered also the parsonage garden, and did everything as tidily as though it had been there.

The night wore on—he did not stop to notice it ; at last the whole bed was delved and trimmed, and the flowers planted—perhaps re-planted, as they would look better still. Thus he worked away through the short hours of semi-darkness, giving a glance from time to time to the little window overhead, for fear some-body might be watching. But neither there nor elsewhere living creature was to be seen ; not even the barking of a dog was heard in the night. At last the silence gave way before the morning; the cock crew, calling up the birds, which one after another arose from their nest in the woodlands, carolling their joyous "good morning" in the dewy dawn.

While he yet stood, or rather knelt, to smooth the earth, he remembered the stories which Aslak had told him in days gone by, and that he once believed that witches and goblins dwelt at Solbakken.

He looked up to the little window, and smiled. What will Synnöve say when she comes to plant her flowers in the morning?——Daylight was fast advancing, and the birds grew more and more noisy. He fled over the hedge, and away. Let any one dare to say it had been he who was over at Synnöve Solbakken's garden, and planted her flowers before the morning!

D

CHAPTER III

THERE were all sorts of reports in the valley, but no one knew anything for certain. Thorbjörn was never seen at Solbakken now, since he and Synnöve had been confirmed, and were no longer considered children; people could not make it out. Ingrid, however, often went over; she and Synnöve also used to go for long walks in the woods.

"Don't stay too long!" the mother would call after them as they went.

"Oh no," answered Synnöve—and did not return till the evening.

The former suitors presented themselves anew.

"She must give her own answer," said the mother, to which the father agreed.

But when Synnöve was taken aside and sounded, there was a flat refusal.

Other wooers followed, but it was never heard that any one of them achieved his luck at Solbakken.

One day, as she and the mother were clearing up the dairy, the latter asked whether her mind was fixed on any one in particular.

It was a sudden question, and Synnövé blushed all over.

" Have you given your word to any one ? " inquired the mother scrutinisingly.

" No !" answered Synnövé quickly.

And there was no further talk on the subject.

But she was considered to be the best match far and wide, and long gazes followed her as she came to church—the only place where she could ever be seen, except at home ; for, the parents being Haugists, she never went to join a dance or any other amusement.

Thorbjörn sat in the pew opposite hers. People never saw them talking with each other, either before or after church, yet everybody seemed to know that there was some under-standing between the two ; but as they did not appear to behave to one another like other lovers in the valley, people talked about them, and all sorts of stories were current. Thorbjörn himself came to be disliked. He knew it, and the very knowledge made him all the rougher when he met with others at some wedding or a dance; no sooner arrived sometimes, than he fell to blows. But his broils grew less frequent, as there were more and more of those who had felt the power of his fists ; and thus Thorbjörn got into a habit of not allowing any one to make himself obnoxious to him.

" You are a man now," said the father, " and you have a fist of your own ; but remember, mine may be stronger yet."

Autumn and winter passed away, the spring was coming, and yet people knew nothing. There were so many stories afloat of rejected suitors, that Synnöve was considered to have a mind of her own. Ingrid was her constant companion. The two also were to go this summer in company to the säter,* for Guttorm Solbakken

* A lonely summer pasture on the Norwegian hills, at a distance sometimes of many miles from the farm itself. Usually one of the daughters goes with the cattle to the säter, and there she spends the summer months in a humble cottage ; seeing no one, except, perhaps, at times her lover, who may think nothing of the distance.

had bought part use of the Granliden hill
pasture. Thorbjörn was heard singing on the
mountain-side, making preparation there towards
the girls' coming.

One afternoon, as he had done his work, and
the evening was closing in upon what had been
a perfect day, he sat down thinking of all that
was being said in the valley. He was lying on
his back, on the ruddy heather, resting his head
in his hands behind him, and looking up into the
heaven as it rose a deep blue dome, beneath
which the tree-tops went swaying to and fro.
The foliage of birch and pine flowed into one
another, forming one heaving cloud, through
which the branches made a fantastic drawing of
their own. The sky peeped in here and there
when a leaf was blown aside, or flowed in like a
sea of blue where the trees stood farther apart.
All this began to move his fancy, and what he
saw took shape.

*　　*　　*　　*　　*

The birch-tree cast laughing glances at the
pine, whose cousin, the fir, looked on in silent
disdain, pricking with her needles about her ; for
with the sunny days many low-born creatures

had sprung up, thrusting their fresh foliage under the very nose of the lordly fir.

"Goodness knows where *you* were in the winter!" yawned the fir, fanning herself, and perspiring resin drops. "What a desperate heat! high up, as we are, in the North— ugh!"

But there was an old grey-headed silver fir, which, having shot up beyond the rest of them, was just able to bend down a many-fingered arm, catching a bold maple by the top till he shivered to his very roots. This hoary old fir had had her branches lopped off by some wood-cutter's axe, and sick of such treatment she took to shooting upwards, till the poor little pine of lower degree asked her humbly whether she was not forgetting the winter storms.

"Forgetting the winter storms?" gasped the towering fir, and reeling with the north wind she sent it flapping round the ears of her frightened relation, which almost lost its balance in the sudden blast. This tall and darksome fir-tree had planted her feet so firmly in the soil beneath, that her toes stood apart at several yards' distance, and even there were stronger than the best branches of the willow, which confided this fact with a certain amount of modesty to the hop clinging to her with enamoured tendrils by the brook. The hoary fir knew the pride of her station, and sailing her branches in the turbulent air, said disdainfully: " Let them lop me now if they can ! "

" No, they cannot now ! " replied the eagle, honouring the fir with a visit ; and folding his kingly wings with dignity, he began to scrape some quite ordinary· sheep's blood from his claws. " I rather think this seems a fit place for the queen—she is troubled, and would wish to lay her eggs," he added softly, looking down bashfully upon his naked claws. Sweet recollections came upon him of early spring days, when all Nature is under the spell of new-born sunbeams, laden with warmth and growth. He soon turned his looks aloft again, gazing from under his feathery brows to the rocky heights where the queen might be found sailing. He burst upwards in quest of her, and the fir could see the couple high up in the clear blue ocean, sweeping along the mountain-tops, no doubt discussing their domestic concerns. The fir opened her boughs, fluttering with hopes ; for, proud as she was, it would make her prouder still to bear an eagle's nursery in her arms. And behold, the royal pair descended in spirals upon the ambitious tree ; they had had their say, and forthwith began to gather sticks and branches. The fir felt herself spreading with swelling emotions —she would grow and spread now to her heart's content ; who should hinder her ?

But a whispering and a talking went through the wood, as the trees perceived the honour done to the mighty fir. There was a dear little birch, bending complacently over the reflecting brook, and whispering to itself that it might well look for some affection from a grey-coated linnet which used to sleep within its branches. She had fanned him with her gentle breezes, and had trapped the pretty flies on her leaves that he might catch them easily ; as the weather grew hot, she had even built a summer-house for him with sprouting foliage ; and it seemed these manifold attractions were not lost upon the linnet. He was just going to domiciliate himself for the season—when lo ! the eagle arrived on the fir above. The linnet had to depart—it was most sad! But he parted gratefully, with a tender love-song to the sorrowing birch, twittering softly that the eagle might not hear.

No better fared a family of sparrows in an elder bush. They had led a dissipated life ; so much so, that a steady thrush close by in a mountain ash was sorely disturbed in her slumbers ; it was no use rating away at her ill-behaved neighbours, they paid not the slightest attention to her feelings, much to the diversion of a dignified fieldfare watching the scene. But now they forgot private quarrels : there was the eagle on the fir-top. They had to turn out—every wing of them—sparrow and thrush and fieldfare. But the thrush swore, as she changed her lodgings, she would never again house herself near a rascally set of sparrows.

Thus the wood was deserted, and stood pensive in the glowing sunshine. Should all its joy henceforth be bound up in the honour done to the lording fir ? That was poor exchange ! The trees grew frightened, and bent to the north wind as it rushed among them ; the big fir above swayed her branches, enjoying the commotion, while the eagle hovered round his nestlings with a happy unconcern, as though it were but a summer breeze laden with incense from the wood beneath. The leafy trees stood mournful; but every branch that bore needles, down to the smallest pine, felt the honour done to the proud old fir, though themselves they had not a nest among them——

"What are you dreaming about?" said Ingrid, as she stepped smiling from between some bushes, dividing them before her.

Thorbjörn rose.

"There is much to occupy one's thoughts," he said, looking defiantly up to the tree-tops. "People talk more than I care to hear," added he, brushing the dust from his jerkin.

"I would not care for people's talk."

"Well, neither should I—yet, after all, they have never said more than I might have made good, had I had a chance of doing so."

"You ought not to say that!"

"Perhaps not"—adding after a while, "but it's true."

She sat down on the grass; he remained standing beside her, looking down before him.

"It won't take much to make me such as

people say I am—why don't they leave me alone ?"

"It will be your own fault for all that."

"Possibly—but other people's too ; I tell you I *will* be left alone!" he almost screamed, looking up to the eagle.

"But, Thorbjörn," said Ingrid gently.

He turned to her, and laughed.

"Don't fret," he said. "Yet there *is* much to occupy one's thoughts— Have you seen Synnövé to-day?"

"Yes ; she has come to the säter."

"To-day?"

"Yes."

"With the cattle from Solbakken ?"

"Yes."

"Who cares!"

"To-morrow we turn out the cattle," said Ingrid, trying to give his thoughts another direction.

"I shall help driving them."

"The father is coming himself."

"Is he?" said Thorbjörn, and was silent.

"He has asked about you to-day."

"Has he?" replied Thorbjörn, snatching

off a twig and beginning to peel it with his knife.

"You should speak more with the father," said the sister kindly; "he thinks much of you."

"Perhaps he does."

"He has much to say for you when you are from home."

"He hasn't when I am there."

"That's your own fault."

"Perhaps it is."

"You should not talk like that, Thorbjörn. You know what he does not like in you."

"What?"

"Shall I say it?"

"I don't care, it's all the same, Ingrid; you know what I know."

"Well—you are too independent; you know he does not like that."

"No—he would like to tie my hands."

"Yes, especially when you use them for blows."

"Shall people tell me what they like, and I take it all quietly?"

"No; but you might shun those whose talk

you don't like ; that's what *he* did, and you know how everybody respects him."

"Perhaps they did not provoke him as they provoke me."

Ingrid was silent for a moment ; then, looking about her, she said :

" There is perhaps not much use in talking— but you know you should not be going where you fall in with them."

"That's the very place which I would not avoid ! I am not Thorbjörn Granliden for nothing."

He had done peeling his twig, now he began cutting it in two. Ingrid, looking at him, said, somewhat hesitatingly :

" Do you know that Knud Nordhoug has come home for his sister's wedding ?"

" I do."

She looked at him earnestly.

" Well, has he more right now to force himself between me and others ?"

"He does not force himself—nor do others wish he should."

"No one can tell what others may wish."

" Yet you know very well !"

"*She* never says so, anyhow."

"How can you talk like this ?" said Ingrid, rising and looking about her.

He threw his half twigs away, and, thrusting the knife into his belt, he said :

"I tell you I am sometimes sick of the whole business. People talk about her as they talk about me, because nothing happens. And for the matter of that, I may not even go over to Solbakken—because the parents don't like it, she says. I mayn't go and see her as other lads may see their girls, because she is one of the saints—now you know."

"Thorbjörn !" said Ingrid, distressed ; but he heeded her not.

"The father will not say a word to help me. 'If you deserve her, you'll get her,' he says. There is nothing but abominable talk on the one hand, and not the slightest assistance on the other. I don't even know that she really——"

With a quick movement Ingrid put her hand over his mouth, looking anxiously about her. Again the shrubs parted, and a slender figure stepped forward. It was Synnöve.

"Good evening," she said.

Ingrid looked at Thorbjörn, as though she meant to say : " Do you see now ?"

But he looked at her somewhat reproachfully. Neither of them spoke to Synnövé.

" May I rest here a while ?" said the latter ; " I have had a good deal of walking to-day."

And she sat down, Thorbjörn turning his head as if to see that the grass was dry where she seated herself. Ingrid's eyes wandered away towards Granliden, and she called out suddenly :

" Dear me, those wretched animals—there is Fagerlin right amid the clover, and Kelleros after her—it is too bad ! high time we should move them to the säter !"

And away she ran after the troublesome cattle, without as much as a good-bye to the two she left to themselves.

Synnövé rose.

" Are you going ?" asked Thorbjörn.

" Yes," she said, but did not move.

"You might stay a little," said he, without looking at her.

" Another time," she replied gently.

" That may be a long way off !"

She glanced up ; he was now looking at her

but it was some time before either of them
spoke.

"Sit down again," he began, half under his
breath.

" No," she answered, and remained standing.

He felt his temper rising. But she was
before him with what he did not expect. Moving
towards him, she said, smiling straight into his
eyes :

"Are you angry with me ?"

And as he looked closer he saw that there
were tears. " No, no !" he exclaimed, passionately, putting out his hand ; but her tears blind-
ing her, she did not see it, and he drew it back.
At last he went on : " You heard what I said ?"

"Yes," she answered, smiling again ; yet the
tears rose faster and faster.

He did not know what to say or do, but the
words came presently :

" I suppose I have been hard upon you !"
This was said most gently ; her eyes fell, and
she half turned away.

" You should not judge what you don't know,"
she whispered so low he scarcely heard it.

He felt very guilty—like a naughty boy he

stood before her, saying meekly : "I beg your pardon."

But that seemed to call up more and more tears. It went hard with him to see her cry; putting his arm round her, he bent his face to hers :

"Then do you care for me, Synnöve ?"

"Yes," she sobbed.

"But it does not make you happy ?"

No answer.

"It does not make you happy ?" he repeated.

Her tears fell faster and faster. She tried to disengage herself from him.

"Synnöve!" he said softly, drawing her closer. She leaned on him and wept hopelessly.

"Come, let us talk a little," said he at last, seating her gently on the heather, and sitting down beside her.

Drying her tears, she meant to smile, but it was a pitiful smile. He took one of her hands and looked into her face.

"Dear Synnöve, why mayn't I come over and see you ?"

She was silent.

"Have you ever asked that I might come ?"

No answer.

"Why don't you ask?" continued he, drawing her hand closer.

"I dare not," she said very softly.

His brow darkened; drawing in his knee he rested an elbow upon it, putting up the hand to his face——

"If this is the case I shall never get over."

Instead of answering she began to pull some heather.

"I daresay——I have done much that may displease——but people should not judge so hardly——I am not bad"—and he stopped, adding after a while : "And I am young——scarcely twenty——I may——," he stopped. "But one who really believes in me——ought——," and then he broke down altogether.

He heard the low voice beside him :

"You should not talk like this——you do not know how much I——I cannot even tell Ingrid——," and she cried bitterly. "I—— suffer——so much."

He caught her in his arms, drawing her closer and closer.

"Speak to your parents," he whispered, "and it will be all right."

"It depends on you," she said gently.

"On me!"

Synnövé turned and put her arms round his neck.

"If you loved me, as I love you——," she said tenderly, trying to smile.

"And don't I?" whispered he.

"No—no! you take no advice from me. You know what would bring us together, but you will not—why not?" And now, having begun to speak, she could go on: "Oh, if you knew how I have waited and waited for the day when I might welcome you at Solbakken! but there is always something that should not be ——and I must be told of it by the very parents from whom I should wish to hide it!"

It was clear to him all at once. He understood now how she waited at Solbakken for the one happy moment when she might lead him to her parents—it was he who made such a moment impossible.

"Why have you never told me before?"

"Have I not?"

"No—not in this way."

She thought for a moment, then she said shyly: "Perhaps I was afraid to tell you."

But the idea that she could be afraid of him touched him so, that, bending over her, he kissed her for the first time in his life.

A change passed over her—the tears stopped, yet something trembled in her eyes; she tried to smile, looked down, then up at him, and now she did smile. Nothing more was said; their hands found each other, but neither ventured to press the other's. She drew hers back gently, and began to dry her eyes and to smooth her hair, whilst he, not moving, looked at her, his heart saying the while: "Well, and if she is less bold than any of the girls in the valley, and if she is to be handled tenderly, no one shall say anything against it."

Thereupon he rose and went with her to the säter, which was not far distant. He would have liked to hold her hand, but he felt strangely forbidden; he thought it wonderful indeed, that he might just be walking by her side.

Feeling thus, he said as they parted:

" It shall be long before you hear again anything about me to trouble you."

.   *   *.   *   *   *   .

Returning home, he found his father carrying
corn from the storehouse to the mill. The
neighbours had their corn ground at the Granliden mill when their own streams ran dry. The
brook at Granliden never dried up. There were
many sacks to be carried, some of ordinary size,
some very large. The women. folk were close
by wringing linen. Thorbjörn walked up to the
father, and took hold of a sack.

" Shall I help you ? "

" Oh, I can manage very well ! ". replied
Sämund, shouldering a load, and walking off
towards the mill.

" There are many of them," continued Thorbjörn, and seized two big sacks ; putting his back
to them, he hauled them over his shoulders,
propping the elbows against them. Half-way
towards the mill he met Sämund returning. The
father gave him a quick glance, but said nothing.
As Thorbjörn, however, came back for a fresh
load, he met Sämund with two still larger
sacks. And Thorbjörn took not more this time

than one small sack. The two meeting again, the father's eye rested on him with a longer look. At last they arrived together by the storehouse. Sämund said :

" A messenger has been over from Nordhoug ; they invite you to join their wedding-party on Sunday."

Ingrid looked up from her washing imploringly ; so did the mother.

" Has there ? " replied Thorbjörn drily, and took hold of the two biggest sacks he could find.

" Are you going ? " demanded Sämund gloomily.

" No."

CHAPTER IV

THE Granliden säter was gloriously situated, with a view commanding the whole neighbourhood. First of all there was Solbakken, amid its woods of many-coloured foliage ; beyond it, and around, lay other farmsteads, each with its boundary line of woodland, looking like so many peaceful spots obtained by human perseverance from the heart of the storm-haunted forest.

There were fourteen homesteads, which could be seen from the Granliden mountain-pasture ; but of Granliden itself only the roofs were visible, and these only by going to the outermost point of the säter boundary. There the girls would sit, watching the smoke as it went up from the chimneys below them.

" The mother is getting dinner ready," said Ingrid ; "there'll be salt-meat to-day."

"Hark ! that's the bell for the men," responded Synnöve, "I wonder where they are at work."

And their eyes followed the smoke as it rose briskly into the clear sunny air, curling up more languidly by-and-by, spreading away over the forest, thinner and thinner, until it dissolved in misty shreds over the landscape beyond.

And thoughts would rise from the hearts of the girls gliding away over the dreamy landscape.

To-day their thoughts turned towards Nordhoug. It was some days after the wedding; but as this festivity would last for a week, they yet heard from time to time the report of a gun, or the hallooing of some powerful lungs.

"They are very merry down there," said Ingrid.

"I don't grudge them their fun," replied Synnöve, bending over her knitting.

"Yet it would not be amiss if one could join it," continued Ingrid, sitting on the heather, and watching Nordhoug, where figures could be seen going to and fro between the buildings, some towards the storehouse, where well-spread tables would be provided, others, in couples perhaps, strolling away evidently in confidential mood.

"I don't know why you should particularly wish to be there," remarked Synnöve.

"Well, I hardly know myself; perhaps it's the dancing!"

To this Synnöve had no answer.

"Haven't you ever joined in a dance?"

"No, never."

"You don't think it would be wrong?"

"I don't know."

Ingrid dropped the subject for the moment, as she remembered that dancing was not approved of by the Haugists, and she would not inquire how far Synnöve might agree with her parents. Her thoughts, however, did not wander far, for she resumed:

"There is not a better partner to be had for a dance than Thorbjörn."

Synnöve hesitated, but assented after a while:

"Yes, so I hear."

"Well, you should see for yourself," suggested Ingrid, with a look at her companion.

"No, I don't wish to see."

Ingrid felt silenced, and Synnövé bent lower to the knitting, counting her stitches. Dropping her work, she said presently:

"I am happier than I have been for many a day!"

"How is that?" inquired Ingrid.

"Oh——well, because I know he is not among the dancers at Nordhoug to-day."

Ingrid looked up wistfully, saying, after a pause:

"I should think some of the girls there will miss him."

Synnövé opened her mouth, but no words came forth; she applied herself again to her knitting.

"Thorbjörn would like to be there well enough, I know that," Ingrid went on, but stopped as the full meaning of what she said came home to her. Synnövé grew red, knitting on silently, till Ingrid, having in her mind gone back over the whole of their conversation, seemed to have discovered a light which made her jump up from her seat in the heather; clapping her hands, she went close to Synnövé, bending down till she could see straight into her eyes. But

Synnövé was engrossed with her stitches.
Thereupon Ingrid laughed merrily, and said :

"You have kept a secret from me all these
days."

"What have I?" replied Synnövé, with an
uncertain glance at her friend.

"It is not exactly Thorbjörn's dancing you
disapprove of," she continued, still laughing.
There was no answer, and Ingrid, laughing more
and more, caught Synnövé round the neck,
whispering in her ears as she did so :

"But you disapprove of his dancing with
others !"

"You are chattering," said Synnövé, disengaging herself and getting up. Ingrid followed
her.

"It is really a great pity, Synnövé, that you
don't dance ; yes, a great pity ! Come, I'll teach
you !"

And she caught her round the waist.

"Teach me dancing?" said Synnövé.

"Yes, and save you from the grief in future
that he should be dancing with others."

Synnövé could not but laugh now ; at least
she tried to laugh.

" Somebody might see us," she said.

"Bless you for this answer, stupid as it is," returned Ingrid, humming already a dance tune, to which she began whirling Synnöve along with her.

"No, no, I can't! let me alone!"

"Nonsense—of course you can! Didn't you just say you hadn't been so happy this many a day? Just try!"

"I don't know how."

"Round and round," said Ingrid, whirling.

"You are so boisterous———"

"Said the cat to the sparrow, when he would not sit still for her to catch him. Come along."

"Well, I would, but———"

"Now, you see, I am Thorbjörn, and you are the little wife that does not approve of his dancing with others."

"But———"

Ingrid went on humming vigorously.

"But———" reiterated Synnöve, and lo! she was dancing.

It was a jumping reel.* Ingrid went before her, taking large steps and throwing her arms,

* A national dance.

76

men fashion; Synnövé followed, stepping gently
and dropping her eyes.

Ingrid sang:

"See the fox, how he watches from under the tree
    In the heather;
And the hare comes hopping so fearless and free
    Through the heather.
See the sun how it laughs in the bright blue sky,
Sending beams aslant from ever so high
    Through the heather.

"And the fox laughs merrily under the tree
    In the heather.
The hare goes hopping in transports of glee
    Through the heather,
And says to himself, 'What a heyday for me!
To dance away, jumping so merrily,
    Through the heather.'

"But the fox lies awaiting behind the birch-tree.
    In the heather;
And the hare arrives jumping quite breathlessly
    Through the heather—
'The fox here! ah, save me, I tremble with fear!'
'I have you,' the fox says, 'how dare you jump here,
    In the heather?'"

"Isn't it nice?" asked Ingrid, stopping quite
breathless herself.

Synnövé laughed, but thought she would rather
be waltzing.

"Well, there is no reason why you shouldn't,"

said Ingrid, and began forthwith to show her how to place her feet, "for," she said, "waltzing is not so easy."

"Oh! I daresay, it will be easy enough, once we have caught the rhythm," replied Synnövé. Ingrid was ready to try it at once—she sang and Synnövé joined, softly first, but getting louder and louder, till Ingrid, stopping short all at once, clapped her hands in astonishment.

"Why! you *can* waltz!"

"Hush, don't tell anybody!" said Synnövé, catching her again round the waist.

"But where *did* you learn?"

"Tra-la-la!" sang Synnövé, whirling her round.

And they danced away merrily, Ingrid singing again :

"See the sunshine dancing with all its might—
Dance away, bright love, it will soon be night !
See the rivulet skipping to reach the great sea—
Skip away, merry lad, for your grave it will be !
See the birch how it whirls in the arms of the wind—
Whirl away, fair maid—is he really kind ?
For see——"

"What extraordinary songs you have," exclaimed Synnövé, stopping.

"Have I ? I really don't know what I am singing! I believe I heard them from Thorbjörn."

"I think they are the Jail-Ben's verses—I am sure they are!" said Synnövé.

. "Are they?" replied Ingrid, rather vexed, and said no more. But presently her eye was caught by something moving along the road beneath them.

"Look—it's somebody from Granliden."

"Is it he?" asked Synnövé.

"Yes, it is Thorbjörn———"

It was Thorbjörn, driving to town. He had a long journey before him, and his waggon was heavily loaded, so he did not hurry the animal; they saw him proceed slowly along the dusty road which lay full in view of the säter. Thorbjörn, hearing voices calling him from above, knew well whence the greeting came; he stopped, and, mounting his waggon, responded so powerfully that it went echoing round the hills. Then the lure came into requisition, and he sat listening to the full tones of the horn being blown to him from the säter till the last sound had died away, when again he shouted in return. Thus it went backwards and forwards, till he felt himself in the happiest of moods. He looked across to Solbakken, and never had it shone so gloriously as in the sunlight now resting upon it.

Sitting there and gazing above him he forgot the horse, which proceeded leisurely after its own mind. But he was suddenly shaken clear of his dreams; the horse had shied with such a violent plunge sideways that one of the shafts was shattered to splinters. Still more frightened, it tore away in wild career across the fields of Nordhoug—for these lay along the road. Thorbjörn jumped up and caught the reins; a struggle ensued; the horse seemed bent on tearing down a steep descent, Thorbjörn trying with all his might to hold it back. He succeeded so far that it reared. backwards, and Thorbjörn flew to the front. Before the horse had had time to make a fresh start, he had secured it, fastening the reins to a tree. The animal had to give in; it stood and trembled; the load had in part rolled off the waggon, and the shaft was beyond mending. Thorbjörn, taking hold of the rein, walked up to the horse, speaking to it kindly to quiet it, turning it at the same time that it might be safe from a rush downhill in case it attempted another plunge. But the terrified creature could not stand still; he had to follow it half running until they found themselves back on the road. And there they passed the thrown goods—the casks were burst open and their contents done for. Hitherto Thorbjörn had only thought of the danger, now he began to consider the consequences, and went into a rage. He saw there was an end to his journey, and the more he thought, the more his passion rose. The poor creature shied again with another plunge sideways: that was too much for Thorbjörn; his fury broke all bounds. Holding the horse with his left hand by the bit, he came down upon its flank with the heavy whip in his right—lash upon lash, mercilessly, till it foamed with agony and kicked with its forelegs against his chest. But he knew how to keep it at a distance, striking away at it with all the force of his rage, making use of the butt-end of his whip now. "I'll teach you—wretched beast!" and down went the whip. The horse neighed with terror and pain —down went the whip. "Ha—you shall feel what a strong fist can do!"—down went the whip. The animal snorted till foam had covered the fist

which yet went on in fury. "This is the first
and last time you shall serve me like that,
abominable beast—there, I'll give it you for it!"
—down again went the whip.

They had turned round and round several
times. The horse resisted no longer, it awaited
each blow trembling, bending its head with a
groan whenever it caught sight of the descending whip. Thorbjörn having spent his rage
gave way to a feeling of shame—his arm
sank. And now he saw, squatting by the
wayside, the figure of a man resting on his
elbows and grinning at him. He scarcely
knew how, but things seemed to grow black
before his face; still holding by the bit of
the horse, he burst with his whip on the
sudden apparition. "I'll give you something
to laugh about!"—the lash descended, but only
half caught the man, who with a yell rolled
over into the ditch beneath him. There he
lay, as he fell, but turning his head he cut a
grimace at Thorbjörn with an ugly grin on his
wry mouth; yet no sound of laughter was
heard. Thorbjörn started back—he had seen this
face somewhere! Yes, indeed—it was Aslak.

Thorbjörn knew not why, but a cold shudder went through him.

"Then it was you who made the horse shy twice over?" said he.

"Well, I was asleep here quite peacefully," replied Aslak, rising; "it was you who woke me, thrashing the beast like a madman."

"It *was* you who made it shy; I never knew the animal that was not afraid of you!" and he turned back to the horse, patting and stroking it as it stood, the big drops of anguish yet running from it.

"It will be more afraid now of you than of me; *I* never ill-treated a beast like that," said Aslak, who had meanwhile risen on his knees in the ditch.

"Take care of your tongue!" cried Thorbjörn, again showing him the whip.

"And don't I take care? Now——where are you going that you are in such a hurry?" added he with a subdued voice, coming up to Thorbjörn, but with unsteady steps, for he was drunk.

"I expect I shall not be going anywhere to-day," said Thorbjörn, trying to disengage the horse from the disabled waggon.

"That is certainly a nasty business," continued Aslak, coming close, hat in hand. "And, goodness me! what a mighty fine fellow we have grown since I last had the pleasure of seeing you!"

Aslak stood by as firmly as his staggering feet would let him, hiding his hands in his trouser pockets, while Thorbjörn was still busy about the horse; he could not get it free; he needed assistance, yet could not bring himself to ask it of Aslak. Aslak, indeed, presented an ugly appearance; his clothes were covered with mud from the ditch; his hair was matted and glued together, hanging in unyielding masses from beneath a battered hat. His face, although in a measure it had the well-known features of former days, now wore a continuous grin, and the eyes were even more closed than they used to be; so much so, that he held the head backwards with parting lips as he attempted to look at people. His features had grown powerless and his limbs had stiffened, for Aslak led a drunkard's life. Thorbjörn had occasionally met him before, but Aslak pretended to know nothing about it. · He went hawking about the country, and was always to be found when a wedding or other festivity was coming off; for then he could sing his songs and tell his stories as indeed only he knew how, receiving his pay in drink. Thus also he had come to the wedding at Nordhoug, but, as Thorbjörn learned afterwards, had seen it advisable to withdraw his person for a while, having, according to his old habit, worked people into a frenzy, and not wishing himself to take the consequences of their rage.

"You might as well try to set the horse somehow to the waggon instead of disengaging it," said he. "You'll have no choice but go down to Nordhoug and get things mended."

This thought had already presented itself to Thorbjörn, but he had turned from it.

"They are at their wedding now," said he.

"And lots of people to assist you," added Aslak.

Yet Thorbjörn was undecided. Without help, however, he could move neither forward nor backward, and nothing seemed left but to go to the nearest farm. Slowly he secured the horse to the broken vehicle and turned away in the direction of Nordhoug. Aslak followed. Thorbjörn after some time looked back at him.

" I return to them in fine company," said Aslak, grinning.

Thorbjörn did not answer, but strode ahead ; Aslak staggered after him singing :

"They two set out to a wedding feast," &c., the beginning of a song.

" You are in a hurry," he remarked presently ; " you'll be there before you know where you are."

Thorbjörn remained silent. Soon the sounds of dance music grew distinct, and from the windows of the great two-storied building faces looked forth to watch the approaching figures. Others collected in the farmyard, and Thorbjörn saw that they talked gesticulating, evidently exchanging their notions as to who might be coming. Presently he perceived he had been recognised, also that they discovered the ruin of his team, and noticed the fragments of his waggon-load about the fields. The dancing stopped, and the whole of the wedding-party came swarming through the doorway just as the two arrived in the farmyard.

" Here we are, wedding guests against our will," said Aslak, approaching the party behind Thorbjörn.

Thorbjörn was welcomed by all ; they gathered around him, expressing their pleasure at seeing him.

" Blessings on the happy day ; good beer on the table, pretty girls on their feet, and a fine fiddler to scrape away," said Aslak, burrowing among the people.

Some laughed, others did not, and one said, "Aslak will die with a joke some day."

Thorbjörn soon discovered old acquaintances, who inquired into his mishap. He was not allowed to go back himself to his horse and scattered goods ; others were sent to manage for him. The bridegroom, a young man, and formerly one of his schoolfellows, invited him to try the wedding beer, and they went to the house. Some—especially the girls—wished to go on dancing ; but others proposed to rest, and since Aslak had come back, to get him to tell one of his stories.

" But mind you make a better choice than your last ! " said one, giving Aslak a thump.

Thorbjörn asked what had become of the rest of the young men.

" Well," replied one, " they got at loggerheads a little while ago ; some have gone to lie down, others are on the threshing-floor playing at cards, others again are keeping company with Knud Nordhoug."

Thorbjörn did not inquire where Knud Nordhoug was to be found.

The father of the bridegroom, an old man sitting quietly with his pipe and a can of beer, now said :

" Well, Aslak, let's hear ; I suppose we'll all be listening once you have begun."

" Are there others to join in the request ? " asked Aslak, having taken a low seat at some distance from the company.

" Yes," replied the bridegroom, " I do."

" Are there yet others to ask me in this way ? " continued Aslak.

" Yes," said a young woman, coming up from one of the benches in the background with a jug of wine ; " this is the way to ask you."

It was the bride, a young woman of about twenty, fair-haired, but of somewhat spare person, with big eyes and a forbidding expression about the mouth. "*I* like the stories you tell," she added.

The bridegroom looked hard at her, and his father at him.

"Yes, these people of Nordhoug have always liked my stories," rejoined Aslak. "I drink to their health!" and he emptied the glass which one of the young men had handed him.

"Now let's hear," called out several voices.

"Let us have the story of Sigrid, the gipsy girl," proposed one.

"No, that is an ugly story," objected others, especially female voices.

"Shall it be the Battle of Lier?" suggested Svend, the drummer.

"No, something merry!" interposed a young man, tall and lanky, leaning in his shirt-sleeves against the wall, while his right hand, dangling lazily, played rather familiarly with the hair of two young girls sitting near him—they scolded, but did not move away.

"I shall just tell the story I like," decided Aslak.

"The devil you will!" grunted an old man,

lying on a bed smoking, one of his legs dangling carelessly, while with the other he kicked against the bed-post, where a jerkin hung suspended.

" I'll thank you to leave my coat alone," said the young man leaning against the wall.

" I'll thank you to leave my girls alone," retorted the old man.

Then the damsels moved from their seat.

" Yes, I just tell the story I like," repeated Aslak. " As I gulp down the brandy, my courage comes handy," and he clapped his hands.

" You shall tell what *we* like," continued the old man from the bed, " for it's *our* brandy."

" What d'ye mean ? " demanded Aslak, with expanding eyes.

" I mean, the pig which we fatten is ours," explained the old man, his leg still dangling.

Aslak closed his eyes, remaining silent, his head hanging sideways ; presently it sank to his chest.

They talked to him ; he seemed beyond hearing.

" It's the drink," said some.

At these words Aslak looked up smiling.

"I have got a story now," said he ; " oh, and it's a merry story," he added, laughing open-mouthed, but no one heard his laughter.

"It's one of his gay moods," rejoined the father of the bridegroom.

"It costs nothing to nobody," continued Aslak, putting out his hand ; "just one more drop to a weary traveller!"

His request was complied with. He emptied the glass slowly, retaining the last drop on his tongue as if loth to part with it ; but swallowing it eventually he turned to the man on the bed, saying, "Now, let's hear your pig!" Folding his hands over his knees, swaying his body to and fro, he began :

"There was a girl, and she lived in a valley. The valley had a name, but that does not matter. The girl was a beauty, and so thought the wealthy peasant—d'ye perceive ?—and she was a servant in his house. She got good wages, yes, and more than she ought to have had : she got a child. Some said it was the peasant's, but he didn't say so, for he had a wife. And she didn't say so, for she was proud, poor creature. Thus it happened that it was christened with a lie, and

as that child of hers turned out to be a great
good-for-nothing, it didn't much matter about the
lie.   She was housed at the bottom of the farm,
and of course the wife did not like that.   If the
poor girl ventured up to the house she threw the
broom at her; and if the poor wretch of a boy
tried to play with the children they were told to
kick him away,—he was but a bastard, said the
wife.   Day and night she worried her husband
to send the brat's mother away.   He refused
while he was a *man;* but he began drinking,
and then the wife got the upper hand.   The
poor girl had a miserable life of it, worse and
worse as the years went on, and she almost died
for hunger with her boy, who *would* not leave
his mother.

"Eight years came and went, and yet the
girl was at the farm ; but now she should go!

"And indeed she did go———but just the very
night before, the farmhouse burned up in the
most delightful way ; the house was burnt and
the rich peasant was burnt, for he was drunk.
The wife saved herself and the children, and
she said the wretched creature had done it.
Perhaps she had———perhaps she had not, who

knows ?———That boy of hers was a queer fellow.
For eight years he had seen his mother starving
and weeping, and he knew how it was ; for she
had often told him when he asked her why she
was always crying. She cried and told him the
very day before she was to be turned from the
farm ; and that, no doubt, was the reason why
the boy was from home that night———but *she*
was put into prison for life, for she herself told
the judge that *she* had lit up the lovely fire that
night. The boy remained in the neighbourhood, and people gave him to eat, because he
had such a wicked mother. By-and-by he went
into another valley, where people were not so
kind to him, for they did not know about his
wicked mother, and he, you see, didn't tell them.
———When I last met him he was desperately
drunk, and people say he is nearly always drunk
now. If this be true or not, I don't care ; but
I can't for the life of me see what better he
could do. He is a terribly wicked fellow, you
may be sure. He can't bear—*can't bear* that
people should be good to one another ; and still
less does he like them to be good to him. He
would like everybody to be just as miserable as

he is—but he only says that when he is drunk. And then he weeps—weeps—weeps, just about nothing ; why, what should he be crying about ? He has never stolen a brass button in his life, nor done any of the wicked things others do, so there is nothing for him to cry about. And yet he weeps—weeps—weeps. You should just see him in his awful tears ; but don't believe they are real, for he only cries when he is drunk, and then, of course, he can't help it."

Aslak stopped here, breaking into a paroxysm of tears and falling from his chair ; but calming down very soon as he fell asleep.

" The pig is drunk," said the man on the bed ; " he always cries himself to sleep."

"That was an ugly story," remarked the listeners, especially the womankind ; they rose to go out.

" I never heard him tell other than ugly stories when he had his way," said an old man, rising from his seat by the door. " Heaven knows why people like to hear them," he added, with a look at the bride.

CHAPTER V

Some went out, others looked for the fiddler to begin dancing afresh; but the poor fiddler was lying asleep in a corner, and some, having pity on him, begged to let him rest.

" For since the other fellow, Lars, has been knocked down, this poor Ole had all the fiddling, day and night."

Thorbjörn's horse and his broken goods had meanwhile been brought to the farm; the horse was being put to another waggon, as no entreaties seemed to prevail with Thorbjörn to remain. The bridegroom especially pressed him to stay.

" Things are not quite so happy here as you might expect!" said he.

Thorbjörn, struck by these words, grew meditative, but insisted he must leave before the evening. The guests, perceiving he would not remain, dispersed. There were many people, but somehow the place looked gloomy and not exactly in wedding gear. Thorbjörn set himself to mend his harness, and required some wood. There was none in the yard, so he went farther to a shed where the firewood was kept, walking slowly and thoughtfully, for the bridegroom's words had set him thinking. Having found what he wanted, he sat down lost in thought, the knife in one hand and a chip in the other, when his reverie was suddenly broken into by a groan close by. It seemed to come from the other side of the thin partition wall, from the adjoining waggon shed. And Thorbjörn listened.

"Is it——you——really?" a voice—unmistakably a man's—said slowly and with evident effort. He heard weeping, but that was not a man's voice.

"Why did you come?" was asked presently, with accents almost stifled by tears.

"Whose wedding could I more fitly fiddle at than yours?"

"It's evidently Lars, the fiddler, who, they said, had been knocked down," thought Thorbjörn. "But the other? it must be the bride herself!"

Lars was a tall handsome fellow, whose old mother lived in a small cottage belonging to the Nordhoug farm.

"Why did you never speak?" said she, huskily and slowly; she seemed greatly excited.

"I did not think it was necessary between you and me," was the curt reply.

There was silence. Presently she resumed:

"Yet you knew that *he* was seeking my hand!"

"I gave you credit for holding your own."

There were renewed tears—and again she broke out:

"Why did you never speak?"

"Much would have been the use for the son of old Bertha to propose for the daughter of Nordhoug," was answered, amid gasps and groans. He waited for a reply.

It came slowly: "Have we not looked to one another this many a year? but——"

"You were always proud, a fellow didn't dare to speak——"

"And yet there was nothing I desired more earnestly——I waited—waited day after day ——when we met about the place——till felt

97   G

sometimes as though I were offering myself. At
last I thought you despised me."

Again there was silence. Thorbjörn heard no
answer, no sobbing, not even the sick man's
breathing.

He thought of the bridegroom, whom he
believed to be an honest fellow, and he pitied him.

At last she spoke again :

" I fear he will have little joy of me——
he——"

" He is an honest man," said the poor fiddler,
groaning. No doubt his chest pained him. She
seemed to suffer with him, for she said :

" It will be very hard now for you——but
——I daresay we should never have come to
speak out if this had not happened. When I
saw you at blows with Knud, then only I understood you."

" I could not bear it any longer," said he ;
adding after a pause——" and Knud is a bad
man."

" Well, he is not good," replied the sister.

They were silent again. Then he resumed :

" I wonder if I shall recover from this——it's
all the same to me ! "

"If you are unhappy, I am much more so," and she wept passionately.

"Are you going?" asked he presently.

"Yes," she replied; and again—"O good God! what a life it will be!"

"Do not cry so," said he. "God will soon put an end to my life, and then, you'll see, things will go better with you."

"Oh why—why did not you speak?" repeated the stifled voice, broken by tears.

Thorbjörn thought she must have left after this, or else was quite unable to speak again. He heard no more, and went his way.

"What was there between the fiddler and Knud Nordhoug to bring them to blows?" inquired Thorbjörn of the first he met in the yard.

It was Peter, the farm servant; but he only puckered up his face as if to hide something in its wrinkles, saying: "You may well ask, it was just nothing. Knud merely inquired of Lars whether his fiddle was in good tune for this wedding!"

At this moment the bride passed them. Her face was averted, but as she caught Lars' name she turned round, revealing big, red, uneasy eyes. The rest of her face was cold, so cold that Thorbjörn could not reconcile it with the words he had just heard, which again set him thinking.

At the farther end of the farmyard the horse stood waiting for him. He fixed the harness, and then looked round for the bridegroom, in order to bid him good-bye; he did not particularly care to go in search of him, feeling it rather a relief not to see him anywhere about, and mounting his waggon he prepared to drive off. At that moment, however, a calling and shouting arose from the great barn at the other side of the yard; a noisy party burst from it headed by a big fellow, and Thorbjörn understood the words:

"Where is he——is he hiding? where? where?"

"There! there!" was shouted in return.

"Don't let them meet!" called out others. "There'll be mischief."

"Is that Knud?" asked Thorbjörn of a little boy close to his waggon.

"Yes, he is the worse for drink, and then he never rests till he has had a quarrel."

Thorbjörn had hold of the reins, and called to the horse to start.

"Don't go! stop there!" It was Knud coming near.

He pulled at the rein, but the horse not answering, he let it go.

"Stop! stop! are you afraid to stop, Thorbjörn Granliden?" he heard now close behind him. Again he pulled, without, however, looking back.

"Get down and keep us company!" said one of the party.

Thorbjörn turned his head:

"No, thank you, I must go home!"

But they tried to dissuade him from going. The whole band had by this time gathered round the waggon. Knud put himself at the horse's head, stroking it first and then taking hold of the bridle, as if to examine its face. He was a tall lanky fellow, with fair but bristling hair, and a pug nose. The mouth was large and thick, the eyes blue, but their expression impertinent. He bore little likeness to his sister; some lines about the mouth, however, were like hers, and he had the same straight forehead, though less high.

On the whole, his features were coarse, whilst hers were rather delicate.

" How much do you want for your horse ? " asked Knud.

" I don't intend to sell it," replied Thorbjörn.

" D'you think I could not pay ? " demanded Knud.

" I don't think anything about it—I don't know."

" Do you dare to doubt ? don't let me hear that again ! " said Knud.

The young man who had been leaning against the wall, playing with the girl's hair, remarked now to another fellow beside him :

" Knud does not quite dare."

Knud heard this.

" I not dare ! who says that ? I not dare ! " cried he.

More and more people gathered round the waggon.

" Off now ! Take care of the horse ! " called out Thorbjörn, coming down with his whip and attempting to start.

" Dare you tell me to be off ! " roared Knud.

" I spoke to the horse, I must be off!" said Thorbjörn, without, however, looking at him.

"Don't you see you are driving right over me ? " Knud went on.

" Then go out of my way."

And the horse raised its head high, else it would have knocked it against Knud's chest. Knud caught it by the bit, and the poor animal, remembering the treatment it had received not many hours ago, stood and trembled. Thorbjörn saw it, and it went to his heart, for he felt very rueful about his behaviour to the innocent creature. But his anger rose against Knud. Starting up, he raised the whip, letting it descend over Knud's head.

" How dare you ! " screamed Knud, darting closer.

Thorbjörn jumped from his waggon.

" You are a good-for-nothing fellow ! " said he, getting pale with anger, and throwing the rein to one of the bystanders.

But the old man who had risen from his seat by the door when Aslak had terminated his story, took him by the arm, saying :

" Sämund Granliden is too repectable a man

that his son should come to blows with such a swaggering bully."

This quieted Thorbjörn, but Knud shouted :

" I am no more a swaggering bully than he, and my father is as good as his——Come on !—— It's a pity people should not know which of us is strongest." And he threw off his jerkin.

" They'll soon see," said Thorbjörn.

" They are like two cats," said the man who had been lying on the bed ; " they only half dare—both of them."

Thorbjörn took no notice. Some of the onlookers laughed ; others said it was a shame that there should be so many brawls at this wedding, and worse, that a visitor should be stopped who wished to be off quietly. Thorbjörn looked round for his horse, but the man to whom he had given the rein, had led it away.

" What are you looking out for ? " said Knud insolently. " I don't expect Synnöve is here ! "

" Stop that—she is nothing to you ! "

" O nothing at all ! I don't want to have anything to do with such sanctified people; perhaps it's she who made such a coward of you."

That was too much for Thorbjörn. He looked

round as though taking his measure of the place.
But again some of the elder people interfered ;
there had been enough of Knud's mischief already
at this wedding, they said.

"He shan't harm me," said Thorbjörn, and
they were silent.

Others thought they had looked askance at
one another for a long time ; perhaps they had
better fight it out and be the better friends when
they had done.

"Yes," observed one, "each wants to be first
in the valley ; let's see which is ! "

"Hasn't anybody seen a certain Thorbjörn
Granliden ? " asked Knud, looking round. "I
thought I caught sight of him not long ago."

"Indeed and you have ! " returned Thorbjörn,
giving Knud at the same time such a blow over
the right ear that he staggered back and would
have fallen, but for some of the men behind him.

There was deep silence. Knud caught himself up and flew at Thorbjörn, who stood awaiting him. There was a set-to of some duration ;
each tried to overthrow the other, but they were
evenly matched. Some thought Thorbjörn's fist
dealt most blows, and they fell the heaviest.

" Knud has evidently found his match," said one of the young men ; " give them room ! "

The women dispersed, only one female figure remained on the top of the steps as if to watch. It was the bride. Thorbjörn gave her a look, and stopped for an instant. But perceiving a knife in Knud's hand, he remembered her words that he was not a good man, and with a well-dealt blow he caught him across the wrist, that his arm fell powerless, and the knife dropped from him.

" Well, you *are* a fellow ! " owned Knud, with a yell of pain.

" Am I ? " retorted his antagonist, pressing on to him.

Knud could not well defend himself with one arm, he felt himself caught up and carried along for some distance ; but it was not so easy to floor him. Several times he was dashed to the ground with such force that many another would have given in ; but Knud had a strong back. Thorbjörn carried him on and on, the people starting away, and Thorbjörn after them with his captured enemy, till they had been all round the yard, and arrived again at the door-steps.

There he lifted him once more high, and flung him to the ground with a violence, that his own knees gave way under him, and Knud fell on the flags, the very contact resounding through him. He lay motionless, groaning and closing his eyes. Thorbjörn arose, and looked about him; his eye fell on the bride, who stood without moving.

"Put something under his head," she said, and turned to go into the house.

Two old women passed by. "Goodness!" said one, "there is another on the ground. Which of them is it now?"

"It's—well, it is Knud Nordhoug," answered one of the men.

"Then, perhaps, there won't be quite so many brawls in future," said the second woman. "They ought to keep their strength for some better purpose."

"True," assented the first. "May the Lord teach them to look beyond each other for something above them!"

These words moved Thorbjörn strangely. He had not spoken, but had looked on silently, while others busied themselves about Knud. One and

the other addressed him, but he gave no answer ;
turning away, he fell to thinking. Synnövé rose
before him, and he felt covered with shame.
How should he tell her of this ? After all, the
end of a brawl was less easy than the beginning.
Suddenly he heard his name called, and a " Take
care ! look about !" but before he could turn, he
felt himself caught from behind, and hurled to
the ground. He felt a sharp, stunning pain,
without exactly knowing where. He heard
voices about him, felt the motion of driving,
thought he himself was driving, yet everything
was whirling and uncertain.

It seemed long. It grew cold, but the next
moment a feeling of heat returned, and then
there was a delicious sensation of floating and
floating—all at once he seemed to understand it
—yes, he was being carried beyond the trees—
higher and higher, up to the säter—and higher
still to the topmost mountain. There Synnövé,
weeping, bent over him, and said, he should
have spoken ! She wept bitterly, and said,
surely he must have seen how Knud Nordhoug
had always tried to be before him, and now she
had been obliged to take him. Then she stroked

gently one of his cheeks till it felt quite pleasantly warm, and her tears flowed and flowed over his chest—he felt the running wet.

And lo, Aslak was perching on a stone up there, setting fire to the beautiful trees, and a crackling went through the branches. But Aslak gave only a big grin, repeating: " It wasn't me, it was mother who did it!" And Sämund, his father, was there, and threw the sacks of corn up high, so high, that the clouds caught them, spreading the corn like a mist around; and he wondered that corn could sail about as though it were mist. And looking again at Sämund, he saw him dwindle and dwindle till he was quite small; but yet he could throw the sacks higher and higher, saying : " Outdo me if you can !"

Far away in the clouds was the church, and on the top of the steeple stood the pale woman of Solbakken, with a silk handkerchief of yellow and red in one hand, and a hymn-book in the other. She shook her head, and said : " I won't have you up here till your swaggering and fighting is done with !" And lo! it was not the church, but Solbakken, and the sun was shining from all its windows—his poor eyes could not stand it, and he had to close them——

"Gently, Sämund, gently!" fell on his ear, and he woke as out of a deep sleep, feeling himself lifted and carried. He opened his eyes, and saw he was in the big room at Granliden. A fire burned on the hearth. The mother stood by him, weeping, and the father was lifting him to carry him into the room beyond. But he laid him down again gently.

"There is yet life in him!" said he, to the mother, with trembling voice.

"Lord help us—he opens his eyes!" cried the poor mother. "Thorbjörn, my own, my darling, what have they been doing to thee?" And bending over him, she stroked his cheeks, the hot tears running over him the while.

Sämund wiped his eyes with his coat-sleeve, and, pushing the mother aside gently, he said:

"I had better take him up now." And slipping his right hand carefully under his shoulders, he brought his left arm round him and under his back. "Support his head, mother, if he cannot hold it up himself." And thus they went, the mother's hand under his head, and the father carrying him, into the next room, letting him down gently on the bed.

When they had laid him down, and covered him soft, the father asked whether the farm-lad had gone.

"There he is getting ready," answered the mother, pointing to the yard.

Sämund snatched at the window, opening it, and called out :

" If you're back in an hour, you'll get your wages doubled—never mind about running down the horse !"

He returned to the bedside. Thorbjörn looked at him with big shining eyes. The father looked into them, and his own filled with tears.

" I knew this would be the end," he said softly, and, turning, left the room.

The mother sat on a low stool at the foot of the bed, crying quietly to herself. Thorbjörn wanted to speak, but he felt it such an effort that he remained silent. His eyes, however, were fixed on the mother's face ; she had never seen them so bright, never so beautiful, and it seemed a bad sign.

"May the Lord have mercy on thee!" she said at last. "Sämund will not bear the blow, if you leave us."

Thorbjörn looked at her with motionless eyes and rigid face. His look went through her soul, and she began to pray the Lord's Prayer for him, slowly, for she believed his end was near. And as she did so, the thought rose in her mind, how they all had loved him, and now that he was being taken, none of his brothers and sisters were at home. She despatched a messenger to the säter to fetch Ingrid, and one of the younger brothers who was there with her, and having done so, she returned to her stool at the foot of the bed. He kept looking at her, and his gaze seemed to her like church music, leading up her thoughts to things beyond and above her. Reverently she took the Bible, saying: "I will read thee something that thou mayest feel better:" and having no spectacles at hand, she opened the book at a place which she knew by heart—it was in the Gospel of St. John. She was not sure whether he understood, for he lay as before with a motionless gaze fixed on her; yet she read on, if not for his sake, then for her own.

Presently Ingrid arrived to help the mother, but now Thorbjörn was asleep. Ingrid wept unceasingly ; her tears had begun to flow on the säter with the thought of Synnövé, to whom nothing had been said.

Soon, also, the doctor came and examined him. There was a stab in the side, besides other injuries ; but the doctor volunteered no opinion, and nobody dared to ask him. Sämund, who had followed him to the sick-room, stood with eyes fixed on the doctor's face, and accompanied him to his trap, helping him to mount, but merely pulled his forelock when the doctor said he would call again the next day. He watched him drive off, and turning to his wife, who also had come out, he said—" If he says nothing, it is bad." His lips trembled, his knees shook, and he walked away across the fields.

No one knew whither he had gone. He did not return at evening, nor indeed at night, but only the following morning, and then his brow wore such a look that none dared ask him anything. He himself merely said, " Well ? "

" He slept," answered Ingrid ; " but he is so feeble he cannot even raise his hand."

The father was going to look at him, but turned back at the door of the sick-room; he could not go in.

The doctor came the following morning, and again and again, for days. Thorbjörn could now speak a little, but was not allowed to move. Ingrid constantly sat by the bedside, so did the mother and the younger brother; but he never asked them anything, neither did they address him any question. The father never entered the room, and they saw that Thorbjörn noticed it; for each time the door opened he looked towards it, and his mother and sister thought he was watching for his father. At last they asked him if he was looking for any one.

"Alas! I suppose nobody wants to see me," he replied.

They reported this to Sämund. He listened in silence; but when the doctor called that day Sämund was not at home. As the doctor, however, had left the farm, he met Sämund, who at some little distance from the house sat by the roadside waiting for him. The doctor pulled up, and Sämund asked what he thought of Thorbjörn.

"They have played him an ugly trick," was the short reply.

"Will he get over it?" asked Sämund adjusting the girth.

"The horse is all right," said the doctor.

"The girth is rather loose," said Sämund.

There was a pause, while the doctor looked closely at him; but Sämund was so occupied with the girth he did not see it.

"You asked a little while ago whether he would get over it—yes, I think so," continued the doctor slowly.

Sämund started.

"Then he is out of danger?" asked he.

"He has been so for some days now," answered the doctor.

Sämund's eyes filled with tears; he tried to master them, but they rose again.

"I am ashamed of myself to make such a fuss about the boy," he faltered at last; "but you see, doctor, there is not a finer lad in all the valley."

The doctor was moved.

"Why did not you ask me before?"

"I had not the strength to do it," said Sämund, still struggling with his tears; "and then, you see, the women folk were watching day after day whether I should ask, and I was not able."

The doctor gave him time to calm himself; but Sämund looked at him and said, not moving his eyes from the doctor's face:

"Will he have his health again?"

"To a certain extent, certainly; however, it is too early to judge."

Sämund turned over these words quietly. "To a certain extent," he murmured at last, and his eyes fell.

The doctor would not interfere with his thoughts; there was something about the man which forbade him to do so. Sämund suddenly raised his head—"I thank you for the information," said he, held out his hand, and walked slowly away.

About the same time Ingrid was sitting with her sick brother.

"If you are strong enough to hear it, I will tell you something of the father."

"Yes," said he.

"Well, the first evening, after the doctor had been, the father left home, and no one knew whither he went. He had gone to the wedding people, and everybody there grew frightened as he came amongst them. He sat down quietly and took a drink ; the bridegroom said afterwards he thought the father had taken more than he should.

"Then only he began to inquire about the brawl, and they told him exactly how it had happened. Presently Knud appeared ; the father wished him to say how it was, and took him along to the place where you fought. The whole of the people came out after them ; and Knud told how badly you treated him, and how you lamed his hand. There he stopped, when the father flew at him, exclaiming, 'Thus it happened, did it not?' and lifting up Knud he laid him low on the spot where your blood still reddened the ground. Pressing him down, his right hand unclasped his knife. Knud grew white; no one spoke ; some said they saw the father had tears in his eyes. He did not hurt Knud, and Knud dared not move. The father lifted him up, and again threw him down. 'It is hard to let thee off,' he said, holding him close.

"Two old women passed, and one exclaimed :
'Think of your children, Sämund Granliden.'
And they say the father at once let go his hold
of Knud, and after a few moments was no more
to be seen. Knud slunk away, and did not again
join the wedding-party."

Ingrid had just finished when the door opened
and somebody looked in. It was the father.
She rose and went out as he entered. And so
father and son met again ; what they said to
each other was never known. The mother stood
behind the door, and she thought she once
caught something about how far he might recover
his health again. But she was not sure, and
did not like to go in while Sämund was there.
As he came out his eyes looked red, and he
seemed unusually tender.

"We shall keep him," said he, as he passed
his wife ; " but God only knows whether he will
ever be strong again."

Ingeborg began to cry, and followed her
husband as he went into the yard. There the
two sat themselves down on the steps of the
storehouse, and had much to say to each other.

But when Ingrid returned softly to the bedside, Thorbjörn had a slip of paper in his hand, which he gave to her, saying slowly:

"You must give this to Synnöve as soon as you see her again."

When Ingrid had read the paper she turned away, and cried; for it ran as follows:

"To the much respected maiden, Synnöve, Guttorm's daughter, Solbakken—

"When you have read these lines, all must be over between us. For I am not he whom you should have. The dear God be with you and me.

"THORBJÖRN SÄMUNDSON GRANLIDEN."

CHAPTER VI

SYNNÖVÉ had heard on the second day that Thorbjörn had been to the wedding. His youngest brother had brought the news to the säter. But Ingrid had seen him first, and told him how much he was to say. So Synnövé only knew that his waggon had been thrown, and that he had gone to Nordhoug for assistance ; that he and Knud had come to blows there ; that Thorbjörn had been hurt and was taken home— but it was of no consequence. The news had been told her in such a way that she was more angry than concerned about him ; and the more she thought over it, the more hopeless she felt. What was the use of his making fine promises ? There was always again something which her parents would not like. Yet it should not part us ! thought Synnövé.

It was but rarely that news came up to the

säter—indeed, there was a lapse of several days before Synnöve heard anything further. The uncertainty weighed upon her, and as Ingrid did not return she began to entertain fears. She felt unable to sing the cattle home at night as she used to do, and her sleep became anxious as Ingrid stayed away. Thus she felt weary during the day, which did not ease her load. She tried to get rid of her thoughts by occupying herself. She set about cleaning her milk pails, made curds and cheese ; but she did not work with any zest. Thorbjörn's brother and the boy who helped him with the cattle noticed it, and were sure now that there must have been something between her and Thorbjörn, which discovery gave the boys much food for conversation.

One afternoon, just a week after Ingrid had been called home, Synnöve felt more and more oppressed : such a time had passed and yet no news ! She left off working and sat down on a hillock whence she could overlook the different farms ; they seemed a sort of company now, she could no longer bear it alone. As she sat there, weary and tired, her head sank and she fell asleep ; but the sun was hot and she slept uneasily. She dreamt she was at Solbakken, up in her garret room where she used to sleep. The flowers in the garden sent up a sweet perfume, though it was not the usual smell of the flowers—it reminded her of mountain heather. How strange that is, she thought, and looked out of the window. Thorbjörn was there, actually planting heather. " But, my dear," said she, " what are you about ? "

" The flowers don't do nicely here," said he, working on.

But she pitied the flowers, and asked him to bring them up to her.

"Certainly," he said, gathered them together, and went in to her. She was not in the garret room now, for he could walk in straight from the garden. And the mother, too, came in.

"For heaven's sake ! I won't have that dreadful Granliden boy come to see you!" exclaimed she, barring the way.

But he would not be stopped, and the two confronted each other.

" Mother ! mother ! it's only my flowers he is bringing !" pleaded Synnöve, sobbing.

" Flowers indeed!" said the mother, holding out her arms to prevent his approach.

Synnövé grew frightened; she did not know which of the two she would like to get the upper hand; she did not wish either to succumb. "Oh, take care of my flowers!" but they heeded her not; they were actually fighting now, and the pretty flowers were thrown all about the floor. The mother trod on them, and so did he. Synnövé cried, and it seemed to her that no sooner had he yielded up the flowers than he grew ugly, very ugly! His hair spread out in knotty tangles, his face grew terribly large, and he had actual claws to his fingers, with which he tried to seize the mother. " Take care, mother— take care! don't you see, it is not he at all, it is another!" She wanted to go near the mother to help her, but could not move from her place. She heard her name being called—again and again. Thorbjörn rushed away and the mother after him. Again she heard herself called.

" Yes," she said, opening her eyes.

" Synnövé," the voice repeated.

" Yes," she answered, looking up.

" Where are you ? "

"Why, it's the mother herself calling me," said Synnövé, starting up, and going to the outer hedge of the säter—there the mother stood with a basket, looking at her.

"You don't mean to say you were asleep in broad daylight, and out of doors!"

"I was so tired," replied Synnövé, "I could not help lying down, and I dropped off without knowing it."

"You should not do so, my child!——Here, I have brought you something in the basket ; I was baking yesterday, as the father had to go on a journey."

But Synnövé felt that the mother somehow had another reason for coming to look after her ; and surely her dream meant something!

Karen, the mother, was, as already stated, a pale fair-haired woman of delicate build and bright blue eyes. She smiled a little when she spoke, but only in addressing strangers. Her features had by degrees assumed a somewhat severe expression ; she was quick in her movements, and never unoccupied.

Synnövé thanked her for coming, and, taking the basket, proceeded to examine its contents.

"You may do that by-and-by," said the mother. " I see that your milk pails are not yet cleaned. Work first, my child, pleasure and rest afterwards."

" Yes, mother, it is only to-day that the work remained half-done."

" Well, as I am here, I may as well help you," continued the mother, tucking up her skirt. "You must always use yourself to tidiness, whether I am here or not." She led the way to the dairy, Synnöve following. The pails were taken out and washed. The mother examined everything, gave an admonition where it seemed needful, was herself heart and soul in the cleaning process, and thus several hours passed by. During their work she told Synnöve how things went at home, and how much she had had to do to get the father ready for his journey. Then she inquired whether Synnöve read her Bible regularly before going to bed at night. " Never forget that," she said, " else your work will not prosper the next day."

Everything done, they went out and sat down on the low grass to await the cows coming home. Presently the mother asked whether Ingrid would

not be returning soon to the säter. Synnövé
knew no more about it than the mother did.
" That's their going on," continued the mother,
and Synnövé knew well enough it was not
Ingrid she referred to. She tried to turn the
conversation, but had scarcely courage to say
anything.

" The Lord visits those who do not bear Him
in their hearts, and He comes when they least
expect it," said the mother.

Synnövé was silent.

" I always said the fellow would come to
nothing——such disgraceful conduct—it's shame-
ful ! "

Both looked down into the valley, taking great
care not to meet one another's eyes.

" I hear it is very bad," the mother went on.
Synnövé's chest heaved.

" Is there any danger ? " asked she.

" Well——there is the stab in the side, and
other injuries besides——"

Synnövé felt the blood rush to her temples.
She averted her face still more, that the mother
might not see it.

" Perhaps there is no real danger," she said,

as calmly as she was able ; but the mother had seen the heaving and gasping, and answered quietly :

" No, there is no imminent danger."

Then Synnöve began to understand that something really dreadful had happened.

" Is he in bed ? " asked she.

" Yes, of course, he is in bed. It is most sad for the poor parents, such honest people. And they brought him up well—the Lord will not require it at their hands."

Synnöve felt so overpowered she knew not how to master her feelings. The mother went on :

" One ought to be thankful that no one had bound herself to him. But, indeed, the Lord always appoints things as they are best."

Synnöve felt so giddy she thought she could scarcely keep herself from falling down the hillside.

" Yes, I always said to the father, We have only this one child, and, please God, we will take care of her. He is a little soft-hearted, the father, though he is a right good man ; and it is well that he knows to take good counsel where he finds it ; that is, in the Word of God."

But Synnövé, thinking of her father and how good he had always been to her, found still more difficulty in swallowing her tears. They rose in spite of her, and she burst out crying.

"You are crying?" said the mother, turning towards her, but she could not see her face.

"Yes——I am thinking of the father——and——," she stopped, stifled by her tears.

"But, my dear child, what is it?"

"Oh!——I don't know——I feel I must cry——if something happened to him on the journey," and she sobbed piteously.

"What can you mean?" said the mother; "what should happen to him? Why, he has the most beautiful road to town——"

"Yes, but just think——how——the other fared," wailed the poor girl.

"The other?——I daresay! But the father does not fly at people like a madman. You'll see him return quite safe, if so be that God does not turn His hand from him."

But these tears, which would not be comforted, set the mother thinking; suddenly she said:

"There are many things in this world which

are hard to bear; but then one should just re-member that there are much harder things still."

" That is sad comfort," replied Synnöve, amid her tears.

The mother dared not say quite all that was in her heart, but she said this :

" The Lord God sometimes directs things quite visibly; no doubt His hand is in this also."

With these words she rose, for the cattle began lowing on the heights above them, the cow-boys blew their horns, and the herd came slowly along ; the cattle had fed, and were con-sequently in peaceful mood. She stood waiting, then she asked Synnöve to go with her to meet them. Synnöve got up and followed the mother ; but it was slow walking.

Karen Solbakken found herself now fully occupied. One cow after another came down ; they all knew her, and lowed for pleasure. She patted them, talked to them, and felt happy among them, seeing their thriving condition.

" Yes," she said, "the Lord forsakes no one who does not forsake Him."

She assisted Synnöve in getting home the

cattle, for everything seemed to go slowly with Synnöve to-day. The mother saw it, and helped her with the milking, although she had to stay longer than she had intended. At last, when the milk was strained and put up for creaming, the mother was ready to go. Synnöve prepared to go with her part of the way.

"No, no!" said the mother. "I daresay you are tired and need rest now." And, taking the empty basket, she held out her hand, saying, as she looked straight in the girl's eyes, "I will come again soon and see how you get on——— Hold by us, and do not think of others."

The mother had barely left when Synnöve began to turn it over in her mind how she might quickest get a message to Granliden. She called Thorbjörn's brother to send him; but when he came she was frightened to trust herself to him, and said she had called him by mistake. Then she thought of going herself. For certainty she must have, and it was not nice at all of Ingrid to leave her altogether without news. It was a beautiful clear night, and the distance was not so great that she could not have gone, drawn thither as she was by such a matter.

As she sat considering, everything came back to her that the mother had said, and her tears flowed afresh; and now she could hesitate no longer. Throwing a shawl about her, she went stealthily that the boys should not perceive it.

The farther she advanced the more she hastened her steps, and soon she fell into a running, so that small stones were sent rolling down the path, frightening her with the sounds thus occasioned. Although she knew it was merely the patter of stones, she yet had a feeling as if some one were near. She stood to listen; no, there was nobody. On she went again, even faster than before, till she trod upon a large stone sticking loosely in the ground; but giving way now, it descended noisily down the hill, carrying earth and branches along with it. There seemed to be noises all about her, and again she stood frightened, growing still more alarmed when she perceived a figure rising and moving on the road below. She thought first it was some wild animal, and stood with bated breath; but the figure also stopped, sending up a "Who's there?" It was the mother.

Synnövé's first action was to jump beside the path and hide in a bush. She listened anxiously, fearing the mother had recognised her, and would be coming back, but she did not. She waited, that the mother might get to safe distance ; and when she went on herself it was cautiously ; yet she reached Granliden before long.

She felt her heart beating when she saw the farm before her, and the nearer she came the more it beat. All was still. Some farming utensils stood against the wall, firewood lay piled up for use, and the axe was stuck firmly in the block. She went through the yard to the door, where she paused. No sound was to be heard ; and as she stood meditating whether she would go up to Ingrid's garret room, the thought struck her it would have been just such a night when, all those years ago, Thorbjörn came over to Solbakken to plant her flowers. Taking off her shoes with a quick movement, she went softly up the stair.

Ingrid was not a little frightened when she roused and saw it was Synnövé who had waked her.

" How is he ? " whispered Synnövé.

Then Ingrid understood. She wanted to rise and dress first, to avoid a direct answer; but Synnövé sat down on the bed, and, begging her to lie still, repeated her question.

"He is better now," replied Ingrid in a whisper. "I daresay I shall soon be back to the säter."

"Dear Ingrid, do not hide anything from me. You cannot tell me anything so bad that I had not feared worse."

Ingrid still tried to soften her answers; but Synnövé gave her no time to consider her words. There were whispered questions and whispered answers, rendered more awful still by the deep silence all around—one of those solemn moments when one dares to look even the most terrible truth straight in the face. One thing was beyond doubt with both, that Thorbjörn's guilt, if any, was very small indeed, and that no wickedness of his rose between them and their love for him. Both cried much, though very softly; Synnövé's tears, however, came deepest. She sat on the bed shaken to her inmost soul.

Ingrid tried to comfort her, reminding her of all the pleasant hours they three had had together. She meant to give her something cheerful to think about, but she only succeeded in making matters worse ; for every little recollection of bygone days seemed a fresh cause for despairing tears.

" Has he asked after me ? " whispered Synnöve.

" He scarcely speaks at all."

But Ingrid remembered now the slip of paper, and it lay heavy on her heart.

" Can he not speak ? "

" I hardly know——Perhaps he thinks the more."

" Does he read ? "

" The mother read to him the first day, and now he looks for it every day."

" What does he say ? "

" Well, you see, hardly anything ; he just lies quiet."

" Is he in the painted room ? "

" Yes."

" Looking towards the window ? "

" Yes."

Both were silent ; then Ingrid began again :

" The little whirlabout you once gave him hangs at the window, where he sees it."

"Well, I don't care," said Synnövé suddenly, with determination; "no one in the world shall make me give him up now, happen what may."

Ingrid drew a deep breath.

"The doctor does not know if ever he will be quite well again," she whispered.

Synnövé raised her head, forcing back her tears, and looked at Ingrid without saying a word. Dropping her eyes, she sat thoughtful; the last slow tears trickled down her face, but no fresh ones followed. She folded her hands and sat motionless, as though she were taking a great resolution; then with a sudden smile she bent over Ingrid, giving her a long and loving kiss.

"If he is helpless, I will nurse him. I shall now speak with my parents."

These words pained Ingrid's heart; but before she could find an answer Synnövé seized her hand, saying:

"Good-bye, Ingrid! I'll go back by myself;" and she turned to leave.

"There is a bit of paper," whispered Ingrid.

"A bit of paper?" repeated Synnövé.

Ingrid was up now looking for it, and as her

left hand placed the little note into Synnövé's
bosom, her right arm stole round her friend, to
whom she now paid back her kiss. Synnövé
felt big hot tears drop on her face. Then Ingrid
led her gently out of the room, locking the door
behind her. She dared not look at what was to
follow.

Synnövé went downstairs softly in her stock-
ing-feet. But many thoughts were busy within
her ; she made a heedless noise, grew frightened,
and ran with the shoes in her hand past the out-
houses to the little wicket-gate beyond. There
she stopped to put on her shoes, and then went
away with rapid strides up the hill. Humming
some tune to herself, she walked faster and
faster, till she grew tired and had to sit down.
Then only she remembered the slip of paper.

*   *   *   *   *

The next morning, when the dog began to
bark and the boys awoke, when the cows should
be milked and let out, Synnövé had not returned.

As the boys stood wondering what could have
become of her, for they had discovered that her
bed had remained untouched that night, Synnövé

herself appeared. She was very pale, and said nothing. Quietly she prepared the boys' breakfast, put provisions for the day into their bags, and set about the milking.

The mist hung heavy on the lower mountain ridges, the ruddy pasture lay sparkling with dew; it was cold, and the dog's barking echoed clear and crisp from the heights. The cows were let out; each greeted the fresh morning air with a long-drawn low, and made away for the meadow-gate. But there the dog sat watching, and allowed none to pass till all were ready, then he made way for the herd. The tinkle of their bells went forth like a stream of sound over the hills, the dog's barking shook the quiet air, and the boys blew merrily through their shepherd's horn.

Synnöve turned away from all this, turned to the spot where she and Ingrid used to sit, looking down upon the valley. Her eyes were tearless; she sat very still, looking into the waking landscape, and hearing from time to time the different sounds which blended in harmony the more distant they became.

Presently she began singing to herself, softly

at first, but louder and louder, breaking into clearer sounds as the song took shape, following another which she had known since she was a child.

"I thank thee for all that now is past,
  The happy hours of childhood's play
I thought it thus would for ever last
  And gild every coming day.

"I thought these hours would twine a bond
  From the silvery birch-tree where we played
To the happy home, and still beyond,
  Till near the church we are laid.

"How many an evening I waited for thee,
  My longing eyes o'er the Firside would roam;
But the shadows sunk low on the willow-tree,
  Thou found'st not the way to my home.

"Yet my fainting heart on trust would rest:
  'Thou wilt come if I patiently wait for thee!'
But the days would rise and go to the west—
  Thou cam'st not to comfort me.

"It is hard for the poor and longing eye
  To turn away from its long-loved home;
It has but a tear, and the heart but a sigh—
  But where shall it henceforth roam?

"The place where yet there is hope to be found,
  They say, is the peaceful church on the hill;
Yet even there my heart would be bound,
  It would meet him and think of him still.

"I know not why God should have brought us so
   close,
   Why the homestead should neighbour each other
   so well,
Why each of the other, where'er each goes,
   Should hear, I cannot tell!

"I know not why even the church should say:
   There's a bond that remains between you still!
We knelt there together the self-same day,
   One blessing our hearts did fill."

CHAPTER VII

IT was some time after these events that Guttorm and Karen sat one day in the large sunlit room at Solbakken, reading to each other out of some new books which had but lately come from the town. They had been to church in the morning, for it was Sunday; and then they had made the round of the place to see how the harvest was getting on, and to consider which fields should in the coming year be allowed to lie fallow and which should be sown. Slowly they went all round their farm, and it seemed to them it had visibly prospered under their hands.

"God knows how things will be when we are no longer here!" Karen had said.

It was then that Guttorm had proposed they should now go in and look at the new books. "One had better not keep thinking of what might happen."

But the new books were soon looked over, and Karen thought the old were best, "for," said she, "people always copy the old ones over again."

"There may be some truth in that," assented Guttorm. "Sämund said to me in church to-day, one always found the parents again in the children."

"You and Sämund had much to talk about to-day, I observed."

"Sämund is a sensible man."

"He seems forgetful sometimes of his Lord and Saviour."

Guttorm did not answer.

"Where is Synnöve?" the mother asked, presently.

"She is in the garret room," replied he.

"You were sitting with her not long ago—how do you think she is?"

"Hm—I should say——"

"You should not have left her to mope by herself."

"Somebody came."

The wife was silent a while.

"Who came?"

"Ingrid Granliden."

"Ingrid? I thought she was still on the säter."

"She came home to-day that the mother might be able to go to church."

"True, she was there——a rare thing for her."

"She has much to see to at home."

"So have other people; but one always manages to go where one would like to be."

Guttorm did not reply, and after a pause Karen went on:

"The Granliden folk were all at church to-day with the exception of Ingrid."

"Yes, it was natural they should wish to accompany Thorbjörn on his first church-going after that long illness."

"He looked still far from strong."

"Better than one could expect. I was astonished to see him look as well as he did."

"Yes; he has paid heavily for his folly."

Guttorm considered, saying presently:

"Yet, he is still so young!"

"There is no real foundation in him——one cannot depend on him."

Guttorm, who sat with his elbow on the table,

his hand fidgeting with a book, fell to reading, his eyes being apparently occupied with the print. Yet, after some silence, he dropped the words :

" They think he will quite recover his health again." Now the mother was taken up with a book.

" That would be nice for such a fine fellow," she said, as though reading it from her book. " May the Lord teach him to make in future a better use of his health."

They went on reading. After some time Guttorm remarked, turning over a leaf :

" He did not look at her once during the whole of the service."

" Yes, I too noticed that he sat without look-ing up till she had left."

" Do you think he will forget her ? "

" It would be best if he did."

Guttorm went on reading, and his wife turning over page after page.

" I wish Ingrid would not remain with her such a time," she said at last.

" Synnöve has hardly anybody now with whom she could speak."

" She has her parents."

Guttorm raised his eyes :

" We must not be too hard upon her."

The wife was silent, and then said :

" Well, I never forbade her coming."

Guttorm closed his book, and went to the window, examining the prospect.

" There is Ingrid, going home," he said.

No sooner had Karen heard this than she left the room. Guttorm remained gazing across the fields, after which he betook himself to marching up and down the room. When his wife returned, he stood still and looked at her.

" It was just as I thought," said she. " I found her sitting and crying ; but no sooner did she perceive me, she bent over her chest as though busy with her things." And after some silence she continued, shaking her head : " No, it is not good that she sees much of Ingrid."

Saying this, she began preparing the supper, which kept her going in and out of the room. Synnöve entered while her mother happened to be absent. Her eyes were heavy and red with crying. Passing close by her father, she looked up into his face ; and then sat down at the table, taking up a book, closing it soon, however, as she asked her mother whether she should help her.

"Yes, by all means," was the answer; "occupation is good for most things."

She went to set the table ready. The father, who had been going up and down the room, now stepped to the window and looked out.

"I believe the barley, which the storm had beaten to the ground, is lifting its head again," said he.

Synnövé went up close to him, looking out also. He turned round to her, but as his wife just entered the room, he merely passed his hand gently over her hair.

They supped, but almost in silence.

It was always the mother who gave thanks before and after meals. When they had done she proposed reading and singing—"The Word of God brings peace, and after all it is the greatest blessing in the house." As she said this she looked at Synnövé, whose eyes were fixed on the ground. "I will tell you a story," the mother went on, "every word of which is true, and not without its lesson to those who will take it." And she began:

"When I was young there was a girl at Houg, the grandchild of an old learned burgomaster. He took her early into his house that she might become the joy and comfort of his old age ; and, of course, he taught her the Word of God, bringing her up well in all things. She learned easily, and was soon beyond any of us. When she was fifteen years old, she could read, write, cipher, knew all her schoolbooks by heart, and five and twenty chapters of the Bible besides. I remember her well. She preferred serious occupation to dancing, and one saw her but rarely where pleasure was the object ; indeed, she spent most of her time in her grandfather's garret room, where he kept his many books. If ever we met her she looked as though her thoughts were far away, and we used to wish we were half as clever as Karen Hougen.

"As she was to inherit all her grandfather possessed, many an honest young man was ready to go shares with her ; but she refused them all. About this time the pastor's son came home from the University ; his examination did not appear to have gone off very well, for frolic and dissipation had had more of his attention than his studies, and lately he had even taken to drinking.

"'Beware of him!' her grandfather said. 'I have had much to do with great folk, and in my opinion peasant people are more to be trusted than they.'

"Karen always listened to his advice, and when she happened to meet this pastor's boy she turned from him. But he left her no peace, and wherever she went she met him.

"'You had better leave me alone,' she said; 'it is of no use.'

"He waylaid her wherever he could, so that at last she was caught, and had to listen to him. He was a handsome fellow. But when he said he could not live without her, she grew frightened and ran away. Then he kept watching her house, but she remained indoors. He placed himself before her window at night, but she did not show herself; he said he would kill himself, but Karen knew better. At last he began drinking violently.

"'Take care,' said the grandfather, 'it's all put on.'

"One night he appeared suddenly in her very room. No one knew how he had come in.

" 'I shall kill you!' he said.

" 'Very well; if you have the courage to do it!' replied she.

" Then he began to cry, and said it was in her power to make a man of him.

" 'Could you give up the drink for a whole six months?' said she.

" And for six months he allowed himself not a drop.

" 'Do you believe me now?' he asked.

" 'No, not till you have kept aloof for another six months of pleasure and dissipation of any kind.'

" He did so.

" 'Do you believe me now?'

" 'No,' said she, 'not till you have been back to your studies and finished your course honourably.'

" He did so, and returned ordained for the ministry.

" 'Do you believe me now?' said he, standing before her in his actual vestments.

" 'I should like to hear your preaching,' replied Karen.

" And she did hear him preach the Word,

true and unalloyed as a servant of the Lord's, speaking of his own unworthiness, aud how easy the overcoming was, once the first step in the right direction had been taken, and how sweet the peace of God was, if one had only found it.

" And he went again to Karen.

" ' I believe now,' she said, ' that you will live as you preach. But I must tell you that I have for the last three years been engaged to be married to my cousin Andrew Hougen. You shall put up our banns next Sunday———' "

The mother stopped. Synnöve had not paid much attention at first, but soon she listened with growing interest.

" Is that all? " she now asked, quite excited.

"Yes," said the mother.

Guttorm looked at his wife; she did not meet his gaze, but corrected herself.

"There might be some more———but it does not matter."

" Is it the end of it? " asked Synnöve, turning to the father, who seemed to know the story.

" Well———not quite ; but, as the mother says, it does not matter."

" What happened to him ? " asked Synnöve.

"Well—that is just the point," said the father, looking at his wife. Karen was leaning back in her chair, looking at both of them.

"Was he very unhappy?" asked Synnövé, softly.

"We must stop when we have come to the end," concluded the mother, rising. The father too rose, and Synnövé followed their example.

CHAPTER VIII

A few weeks later all the inhabitants of Solbakken prepared one Sunday morning to go to
church. It was Confirmation-day—it fell earlier
than usual this year—and on such occasions the
houses were locked ; everybody went to church.
They would not drive, for the weather was clear
and bright ; the early morning had been fresh
and windy, but it promised to be a fine day.

Their way lay round the valley and past
Granliden, where it turned to the right, and a
good half-hour's walking beyond would bring
them to the church. The corn had been cut
nearly everywhere, and stood in sheaves; the
cattle had been brought down from the hills and
were grazing in the valley. The meadows bore
their aftermath, and where the soil was poor it
was of a greyish brown. Round about them
rose the many-coloured woods : the birch was

beginning to lose her summer hue; the alder had paled to a sickly yellow; the ash stood shrivelled and brown, but with bright red berries. There had been a several days' rain, and the shrubs along the road, which had been very dusty, were now clean and fresh. But the hillsides began to look upon the valley with gloomy brow; autumn had already swept them bare, leaving them empty and cold; while the swollen brooks, which during the summer had not had much to say, came rushing along with merry noise, foaming and spluttering on their way. The Granliden brook seemed less youthful but more turbulent, especially when it reached the Granliden soil, where the rock which had hitherto accompanied it, hemming in its course, stopped suddenly behind. The forsaken brook gave quite a bound, breaking loose with such a roar that the steady old rock almost trembled, and indeed had a good ducking for its treachery, the brook sending great gushes of water over it. Some curious alder shrubs having ventured too near the precipice, were almost carried off their feet, and stood groaning in the continuous splash. The brook was especially liberal to-day.

Thorbjörn, his parents, brothers and sisters, with the rest of the household, were just passing along this tumult. Thorbjörn was quite well again, and able to help the father with his strong arm. The two were almost always together now, and were so to-day.

"I rather think it's the Solbakken folk," said Sämund, "not far behind us."

Thorbjörn did not look round, but the mother rejoined:

"Yes, it's they——but where is——oh! I see—quite at the back——"

Either the Granliden people now walked faster, or the Solbakken party fell behind, for the distance between them increased till at last they lost sight of each other. Evidently there would be a large attendance at church to-day; the road was crowded with people walking, riding, or driving to church. The horses, well fed in the autumn, and little used to meet in such numbers, were restless and pranksome, which made riding a little dangerous perhaps, but added to the lively appearance of the scene.

The nearer they came to the church the more noisy grew the horses. Each one arriving

neighed loudly to greet those already there, and
these returned the salutation by pulling at their
traces, stamping with their hind legs, and neigh-
ing vigorously. All the dogs of the valley,
which during the week had sat lonely at home,
hearing and perhaps barking at each other,
assembled now by the church, and broke loose
in pairs or packs, fighting and yelping across the
fields. The people stood quietly near the church
wall, talking with one another, half whispering,
and watching each other covertly. The path
along the wall was not wide, and the houses
bordering it on the off-side stood close together.
The women as a rule had the wall, the men
posting themselves along the houses. Only after
they had stood some little time they took courage
to approach each other, and even close acquaintances, catching sight of one another, did not
draw nearer till they considered the proper
moment for doing so had arrived—except perhaps when they had unknowingly been landed
so near each other that an immediate interchange
of greeting could scarcely be avoided ; but then
it was done with half-averted face and few words,
after which each retired to convenient distance.

When the Granliden people had appeared the
general attitude grew even more silent than
before. Sämund did not see many friends, and
passed quickly along the line. Ingeborg and her
daughter, however, were caught at the very
outset. The men had therefore to come back
through the whole row when it was time to go
into the church. At this moment three carts
arrived more noisily even than any of the others,
and drove right among the assembly. Sämund
and Thorbjörn had almost been run over, and
looked up simultaneously. In the first vehicle
they saw Knud Nordhoug and an old man; in
the second Knud's sister and her husband; in
the third their servants. Father and son looked
at each other; Sämund's face was illegible;
Thorbjörn grew pale. As their eyes parted,
they fell on the people of Solbakken, who had
remained behind in order to greet Ingeborg and
Ingrid. But the Nordhoug carts had dashed
between them and broken the thread of their
conversation; they were yet looking after them
and could not easily find words again. At this
moment they caught sight of Sämund and Thorbjörn, who had meanwhile approached and seen

them. Guttorm moved away, but his wife at once looked at Thorbjörn, to discover, if possible, the direction of his eyes. Synnöve, who no doubt had met their glance, now turned round to Ingrid, shaking hands with her, although she had already done so. But suddenly all seemed aware that their neighbours were watching them. Sämund therefore walked boldly across to Guttorm, and said, with averted face : " Thanks for the last !"

" Thanks the same," replied Guttorm.

Then Sämund turned to his wife—" Have thanks for the last !"

" Have thanks yourself," said Karen, not raising her eyes.

Thorbjörn followed his father's example, proffering the same greeting. Sämund had now come to Synnöve ; at her he looked, and she too looked up at him, quite forgetting her " Thanks for the last."

Now it was Thorbjörn's turn. He said nothing, and she said nothing. They shook hands, but without pressure ; neither was able to look up ; neither could move a step. So they stood before each other.

" It will be a fine day," said Karen, looking quickly from one to the other.

It was Sämund who answered : "Oh yes, no doubt ; I see the wind driving away the clouds."

" That will be well for the corn where it yet needs drying," said Ingeborg, beginning to pass her hand down the back of her husband's coat, probably because she thought it needed brushing.

" The good God has given us a fruitful year, but we cannot yet tell whether everything will be safely housed," observed Karen, still watching the two young folk, who continued on the same spot.

" That will depend on the number of hands," replied Sämund, coming round in front of her, so that she could not well see the spot she seemed so anxious to watch. " I often thought things would go much better if some of the farms were to unite their efforts."

"Well, but it might be that both parties wished to secure the fine weather for themselves," said Karen, moving a step sideways.

" No doubt," rejoined Ingeborg, coming up beside her husband, so that even now Karen could not have her eyes on a certain spot; "but then, you see, the corn ripens sooner in some places than in others. For instance, you at Solbakken are always a fortnight before us."

"Yes, we might well be helping each other," assented Guttorm slowly, approaching a step. Karen looked at him. "But there are many things that may upset one's plans."

"Certainly there are many unexpected things," repeated Sämund, but he could not help smiling a little.

"Yes, certainly——" began Guttorm, but his wife interrupted him.

"Human planning is of little avail; the Lord is above it all; things will always go as He sees well."

"It could, however, surely not displease Him if the Solbakken and Granliden folk were to help each other at harvest time," interposed Sämund.

"No," said Guttorm, "it could not possibly displease Him." And he looked anxiously at his wife.

She tried to turn the conversation.

"How many people have come to-day! It

does one good to see them honour the House of God."

No one seemed to have an answer ready, but Guttorm responded presently :

"No doubt the fear of God increases in the world ; more people appear to be going to church now than when I was young."

" Yes, there are more people in the world every year," remarked Sämund.

" There may be many, I suppose most, who only come for the sake of habit," continued Karen.

" I suppose so, especially the young," said Ingeborg.

" The young folk like to meet each other," added Sämund.

" Have you heard that the pastor is thinking of leaving us ? " interposed Karen, again trying to turn the conversation.

" That would be a thousand pities," said Ingeborg ; " he has christened and confirmed all my children."

" And I suppose you would not like him to go till he had married them as well," added Sämund, playing with a bit of wood he had picked up.

"I am surprised the church should not be opened yet," said Karen, looking uneasily at its doors.

"Yes, especially when it is so hot out here," replied Sämund, smiling again.

"Come, Synnövé, let us go in."

Synnövé started, and turned round ; she had been talking with Thorbjörn.

"Wouldn't you rather wait here till the bells begin to ring?" suggested Ingrid, glancing at Synnöve; and Ingeborg added : "We could then all go in together."

Synnövé stood silent, but Sämund turned to her :

"Wait a little while longer and they will be ringing for thee."

And she blushed. The mother gave her a sharp look, but Sämund smiled at her.

"Did not you just say that things happen as the Lord sees well?" said he to Karen. Thereupon he led the way to the church, the others following.

At the entrance there was quite a crowd of people pressing forward to go in ; looking closer they found the doors had not yet been opened.

They were, however, just opening, and the influx
began. But some of the people having gone in,
came out again, thus confusing the arrivals and
separating friends. Close to the church two
men stood talking. One of them was tall and
broad-shouldered, with fair but bristling hair and
a pug nose. It was Knud Nordhoug, who,
perceiving the Granliden party coming nearer,
stopped talking, looking conscious, without, however, moving away.

Sämund, who had to pass him first, looked
at him sternly; but Knud did not drop his
eyes, although he appeared somewhat abashed.
Synnövé, passing next, and finding herself thus
unexpectedly face to face with Knud, grew
deathly pale. At this Knud's eyes fell, and he
turned as though trying to move away. But
the first step brought him straight opposite
to four pairs of eyes—Guttorm's, Ingeborg's,
Ingrid's, and Thorbjörn's. Half dazed, he walked
ahead and stopped short, facing Thorbjörn, who
on his part would have liked to step aside, but
could not for the thronging people. Thus the
two met on the paved approach to the church;
a little above them Synnövé remained standing,

and not far from her stood Sämund, seen by all, and themselves watching the two below. Synnöve's eyes, indeed, forgetful of aught else, were riveted on Thorbjörn's face. Sämund looked from one to the other, so did his wife, Ingrid and Synnöve's parents coming up behind the two. Thorbjörn stood rooted to the ground, feeling the eyes of all upon him. Knud seemed to think he ought to do something, so he put forth his hand a little, yet said nothing. Thorbjörn's hand advanced, but not far enough to meet Knud's.

"Thanks for the last," Knud began, but it struck him this was scarcely an appropriate greeting between them ; he stepped back, feeling guilty.

Thorbjörn looked up ; his eyes beheld the white face of Synnöve watching them. With a great stride forward he caught Knud's hand and said, loud enough for all to hear :

" Thanks for the last, Knud ; perhaps it was good so—for both of us."

Knud gave a sound, something between a gulp and a grunt, trying to speak but could not. Thorbjörn, who had nothing more to say, stood and waited—just waited without looking up or beyond them. But no words appeared to be coming, and as he stood, turning his hymn-book in his hands, it so happened that it dropped from his hold. Knud bent quickly, picking it up for him.

"Thank you!" said Thorbjörn, himself making a movement towards the fallen book. Knud's eyes again dropped to the ground, and Thorbjörn, seeing it, thought: "I had better leave him," and he left him.

The others, too, moved on, entering the church. Having settled in his pew, Thorbjörn looked across to the women; and behold! not only his mother sat smiling at him, but Karen Solbakken's eyes seemed awaiting his look; for no sooner had she caught it than she nodded to him, not once but three times; and, seeing him astonished, she nodded again and yet again with unmistakable approval. Sämund, his father, whispered to him: "That's what I have been expecting."

The introductory prayer was now offered up, and a hymn sung. The boys and girls about to be confirmed were taking their places when Sämund whispered again: "But it will be hard

for Knud to mend his ways. Let Granliden
and Nordhoug be well apart in future."

The confirmation service began. The pastor
stepped to the altar, and the children, rising,
sang the time-honoured confirmation hymn. It
always makes an impression on the listening
congregation to hear the clear, tuneful, and trust-
filled voices of the children thus united—especially on those who themselves have not proceeded so far on life's road as to have forgotten
the day when they themselves had come to the
altar. And such impression deepens when the
pastor—the same, perhaps, for twenty years,
who at one time or another may have stood soul
to soul with each of them—now crosses his
hands on his heart and begins his charge. The
children's tears rise first, as he commends them
earnestly to the parents' prayers. Thorbjörn,
who but a short time before felt himself a dying
man, and even later still had thought he would
remain weak and crippled for life, could not for-
bid his tears, but let them flow unchecked, especially when the children pronounced their solemn
vow of faith and steadfast living—believing, every
one of them, they would keep it faithfully.

Not once during the service did he look across to the women's pew ; but when it was over he stepped to Ingrid, whispering a few words to her, after which he moved away quickly and was lost in the crowd. Some thought afterwards they had seen him turn from the road that would be his way home, taking a path up the hillside instead, leading into the wood ; but no one was sure. Sämund looked for him, but when he discovered that Ingrid too had vanished he gave it up, addressing himself to the Solbakken people ; but lo ! they too were busy asking for Synnöve, whom nobody had seen. Thus it came that each forsaken parent couple went home—each two by themselves. Synnöve and Ingrid meanwhile had hastened on along the path.

" I am almost afraid I should not have come," said the former.

" It can be no wrong," replied the other, " for the father knows."

" But he is not *my* father ! "

" Who can tell ? " returned Ingrid, and then they were silent again.

" I think it is here we should wait," resumed Ingrid presently, when they had reached a spot where the path made a great swerve, bringing them right into the wood.

"His is a longer way to come by," said Synnöve.

"Yet here he is," interrupted Thorbjörn, stepping from behind a great stone.

He had arranged everything in his head what he would say, and that was not a little. And he would have it out all plain and easy to-day, for the father evidently approved—of this he could not doubt after what had happened before church. And besides he had longed all the summer through for just such an hour—indeed it must be quite easy now to say his say.

"We had better go by the wood," he began; "it is the shortest way home."

The girls said nothing, but followed.

Thorbjörn was determined to speak now with Synnöve, but first he thought he would wait till they had reached the top of the hill, then till they had passed the bog; but when not only the hillside but also the bog lay behind them, he fancied it would be better to get farther into the wood.

Ingrid, no doubt thinking that matters were

slow of beginning, fell behind, till by degrees she became altogether invisible. Synnöve pretended not to be aware of it; bending from time to time, she plucked of the berries growing by the wayside.

"It would be extraordinary if after all there should be no talking," thought Thorbjörn, and so he began:

"This is most beautiful weather to-day."

"Yes, indeed," returned Synnöve.

Again they walked on in silence, she pulling her berries.

"It is very nice of you to have come," ventured he at last.

To this she had no answer.

"The summer has been so very long."

Again no answer.

"This will never do!" thought Thorbjörn; "and if we walk on at that rate there will not be any talking." Whereupon he said aloud; "I think we had better wait for Ingrid."

"I think we had," assented Synnöve, and they stopped walking.

There were no berries here which she could have plucked, and Thorbjörn had been aware of this. But she caught up a long stalk, and was busy stringing upon it the berries which she had plucked before.

"To-day reminded me so much of the time when we went to the church to be confirmed together."

"So it did me," she answered.

"Much has happened since." And as she was silent he went on: "But most has turned out differently than we expected."

Synnöve was still bent upon her berries, stringing them anxiously, which kept her head from him. He moved a little, for he wanted to see her face, but she somehow managed to turn it again from him.

He began to be really afraid that he should not manage his say at all.

"Synnöve, I rather think you ought to have something to say—haven't you?"

Now she looked up, and could not help laughing.

"I? What should I have to say?"

This seemed to bring back his courage; he felt bold enough to kiss her; but when he had come close enough to do so, he did not quite dare, and only asked, rather bashfully:

" Has not Ingrid spoken to you ? "

" Yes," she said.

" Then you *have* something to say ? "

She was silent.

" You surely have something to say ? " he reiterated, going quite close again.

" Well, and so have you," she said at last, hiding her face from him.

"Yes," he replied, and would have taken one of her hands, but she seemed more than ever taken up with her berries.

" It is most disheartening that you do not let me speak." He could not see whether she smiled or not, and did not therefore know how to proceed.

"What have you done with that paper ? " he said at last, with determined yet uncertain voice.

She turned in silence. But, following her, he laid his hand on her shoulder, bending now over her.

" Tell me ! " he whispered.

" I burned it."

He caught her face, turning it towards him ; but seeing the tears rising, he again lost courage, and dared not proceed.

"It is strange her tears should come so easily," said he to himself.

Yet as they stood, she found voice to say softly:

"Why did you write it?"

"Has not Ingrid told you——?"

"Yes, but—it was very cruel of you."

"The father thought it right."

"But it was——"

"He thought I should be disabled for life; but now I shall take care of you."

At this moment Ingrid came in sight, and they moved on.

"I never loved you so much as when I believed I should lose you."

"One finds out one's wishes best when one is alone with them," said she.

"Yes, then one discovers who has most power over us," continued he with a clear voice, walking on earnestly beside her.

She had stopped plucking berries.

"Would you like these?" she said, holding out her stalk. He took the hand which offered it.

"Then I suppose it will be best to leave

things as they used to be?" and his voice trembled a little.

"Yes," she whispered, scarcely audible, and turned away.

Thus they went on side by side, and while she was silent he dared not touch her nor speak to her; but he felt strangely elated, till indeed his head turned quite giddy. Everything went dancing before his eyes, and as they reached a height whence they could see Solbakken resting in sunshine, it appeared to him as the spot where he had lived all his life, and he felt drawn to it as to the home of his youth.

"I had better go over with her at once," thought he, growing in courage the more he looked at the place, and strengthening his resolution with every step. "The father shall help me; I cannot put it off another day; it shall be now!" And he marched ahead. All around him glowed in light and sunshine. "Yes, to-day —I'll not put it off another hour!" And he felt so strong—every pulse beating with a power that would carry him straight to the point.

"You are quite running away from me," said a gentle voice behind him. It was Synnöve, who could no longer keep up with his impetuous strides.

He turned ashamed, and went back towards her with outstretched arms, saying to himself: "She shall be my queen—I will lift her high above me!" But when he stood before her, he did nothing of the kind.

"I have walked too fast," he said humbly.

"Yes, indeed," she replied.

They reached the high-road, and Ingrid, of whom nothing was to be seen all this time, appeared suddenly close behind them.

"Now you shall no longer run away from me," she said.

Thorbjörn started; the sister came all too soon. Synnövé, too, felt strangely overtaken.

"I had so much to say to you," Thorbjörn whispered. She could not suppress a smile.

"Well," she said, "some other time." And he took her hand.

She looked into his face, her honest eyes full of a tenderness that sank into his soul, and he thought: "I will go with her at once." But she withdrew her hand gently from his clasp, and turning to Ingrid bid her good-bye. Thorbjörn did not even attempt to follow her.

The brother and sister walked home through the wood.

"Well, have you had your say?" asked Ingrid.

"Of course not—why, there wasn't time for anything!" And Thorbjörn again took to faster walking, as if to avoid his sister's questioning.

"Well?" said the father, looking up from his dinner when the two entered.

Thorbjörn gave no answer, but walked to the further side of the room, no doubt for the sake of hanging up his Sunday coat. Ingrid smiled. Sämund went on with his dinner, but his eyes ever again with a mischievous twinkle rested on Thorbjörn, who appeared immensely occupied with his coat.

"You had better attend to your dinner," the father said at last, "it is getting cold."

"I am not hungry, thank you," replied Thorbjörn, sitting down.

"Indeed?"—and Sämund continued his meal, saying presently: "You seemed in a great hurry after church."

173

"There were folk one had to talk to."

"Well—and did you talk to them?"

"I am not sure," said Thorbjörn.

"Very strange," remarked Sämund, and went on eating.

When he had done, he rose and stood by the window, looking out. Turning suddenly he said:

"Suppose we go and have a look at the fields."

Thorbjörn jumped up, all readiness.

"You might as well take your coat."

Thorbjörn had been sitting in his shirt-sleeves; he now took his every-day jerkin from the wall.

"Don't you see I have my Sunday best on?" said the father.

Thorbjörn therefore resumed his Sunday coat and they went out, the father first, the son following.

They came to the high-road.

"Aren't we going to look at the barley?"

"No, let's look at the wheat first."

Just as they had reached the high-road, a car came in sight.

"These are Nordhoug people," said Sämund, looking up.

"It is the newly-married couple," returned Thorbjörn.

The car came nearer and drew up.

"She is certainly a magnificent damsel this Marit Nordhoug," whispered Sämund, who could not take his eyes from her. She was leaning back on her seat ; a shawl was wound carelessly round her head, another covered her shoulders. She looked straight at Sämund and Thorbjörn ; her powerful yet delicate features were calm as death. Her husband looked pale and worn ; his face bore that expression of peculiar meekness which comes from silent sorrow.

"Making the round of your fields ? " he said.

"We are," replied Sämund.

"The harvest bids fair."

"Oh yes; it might be worse———"

"You are late home," remarked Thorbjörn.

"I had to take leave of so many people after church," said the young husband.

"What ! are you going on a journey ? " asked Sämund.

"I am indeed."

"Shall you be gone long ? "

"Well—rather, I should say."

"And where may you be going?"

"To America."

"To America!" exclaimed Sämund and Thorbjörn, with one voice of astonishment. "A man just married!" added Sämund.

The young husband smiled.

"I expect I shall stay here on account of my foot, said the fox—when he was caught in a trap."

Marit looked first at him, then at the others. A slight flush rose in her face, which yet remained motionless.

"I suppose you take your wife with you?" asked Sämund.

"No, she is going to stay at home."

"They say America is a grand place for making money," interposed Thorbjörn quickly, feeling somehow that a pause might be awkward.

"Oh—yes!" assented the poor husband.

"But Nordhoug is such a goodly inheritance," remarked Sämund.

"There are too many of us," was the answer.

Again his wife gave him a look.

"I shall not be missed," he added.

"Well—good luck on your journey," said Sämund, holding out his hand. "May the Lord give you your desire."

Thorbjörn also shook hands with his old schoolfellow, but said significantly :

"I want a talk with you before you go !"

"It is nice to have a friendly chat with *some* one," returned the other, describing figures with his whip.

"Well, come and see us," said Marit.

Thorbjörn and Sämund looked up astonished; they had forgotten she had such a pleasing voice.

The pair drove away, slowly. A light dust cloud enveloped them. The evening beams shed a lustre around them, setting her gaily-coloured silken shawl in strong relief against his darker clothes ; there was a rise in the road, and the young couple vanished behind it——

Father and son went on in silence.

"It seems to me it will be a long journey for him," said Thorbjörn at last.

"That would seem best," returned Sämund, "if happiness cannot be found at home."

And they were silent again.

177   M

"Why—we have passed the wheat!" exclaimed Thorbjörn presently.

"We can look at it as we return."

And they went on. Thorbjörn did not like to ask whither; for they had left the Granliden fields behind them.

CHAPTER IX

Guttorm and Karen Solbakken had finished their dinner when Synnöve entered, flushed and almost out of breath.

"My dear child!" asked the mother, "where did you remain?"

"I stayed behind with Ingrid," answered Synnöve, beginning to divest herself of a couple of shawls. The father meantime was busy looking for a book.

"What can you have been talking about to keep you such a time?"

"Oh—nothing particular."

"Then you would have done better to keep with us," said the mother, putting dinner before her.

Synnöve sat down, and the mother, taking her place just opposite her, went on:

"Were there some other people, perhaps, who might have been talking also?"

"Yes, there were."

"There can be no harm in the child's talking with people," interposed Guttorm.

"Oh, none—in the least," said the mother. "Yet the child might have walked home with her parents."

There was a pause.

"It was a happy Sunday," Karen began presently; "it does one good to hear the children's earnest promises."

"Yes, and it makes one think of one's own children."

"So it does," said the mother, sighing. "And one feels anxious about them."

There followed a long pause.

"We have much to thank God for," rejoined Guttorm at last—"He has preserved us one child."

The mother sat with downcast eyes, her finger drawing figures on the table before her.

"Yes, she is our one joy," she said, softly; "and she has always been a good girl," added she, softer still.

Another pause.

"Yes, she has always been a joy to us,"

repeated Guttorm ; adding after a while—"May the Lord give her all happiness."

The mother still drew figures on the table. A tear dropped, and the finger went over it.

"Why don't you eat?" asked the father, looking up after this.

"I am not hungry," replied Synnöve.

"But you have eaten nothing," said the mother in her turn ; "and you had such a long walk."

"I cannot eat," said Synnöve.

"Do take something," continued the father.

"I cannot," repeated Synnöve, and her eyes filled.

"But, my child, what is it ?"

"I don't know," she sobbed.

"Her tears come so easily," said the mother. And the father, rising, went to the window.

"I perceive two men coming here," said he after some silence.

"Two men! really?" asked the mother, making for the window.

They both looked out.

"Who can they be?" said Karen, but not exactly putting the question.

" I don't seem to know," returned Guttorm, still looking out.

" It does seem strange."

" It does."

The men approached.

" I think it must be they," said she at last.

" I think it must," assented Guttorm.

The two came nearer and nearer. The elder of them stopped looking about ; so did the younger, after which they continued their walk.

" Have you any idea what they can be coming for ?" asked Karen.

" Not in the least," answered Guttorm. The mother turned, and began setting the table tidy.

" You might as well put on your neckcloth again, dear child ; these men seem to be coming here."

No sooner had she said this than Sämund entered, followed by Thorbjörn.

" God's blessing on the party," said Sämund, standing upon the threshold ; after which he stepped forward with a greeting to each. Thorbjörn did the same. Synnöve stood behind her parents, the kerchief in her hands. She did not appear to know whether she should put it on or not; perhaps, indeed, she knew not she had it in her hands.

"Take a seat," said the mother to the visitors.

"Thank you; we are not tired," replied Sämund, but sat down; Thorbjörn sitting down beside him.

"We lost sight of you after church," remarked Karen.

"Yes, I could not see you anywhere," said Sämund.

"There were many people," continued Guttorm.

"A great many," assented Sämund. "It was a blessed church-day."

"We were just saying so," replied Karen.

"And we said such a day makes one think of one's own children."

. "Just so," said Sämund; "it makes one think of them——and that is one reason why I have come here this afternoon."

Guttorm's, Karen's, and Thorbjörn's eyes wandered about uneasily, as though looking for some object that might prove a safe resting-place, while Sämund proceeded slowly:

"I thought it best to come over myself with Thorbjörn; he would have been a long time about it by himself—indeed, I fear he does not quite know how to help himself in this matter." And he glanced at Synnöve, who, although she saw not, seemed yet to be aware of the look. "The truth is that ever since he has been old enough to think of these things, he has set his heart on Synnöve——and I believe it is the same with her. I am inclined to judge, therefore, it might not be amiss to let them have each other——I did not favour it much while I saw he was not fit to guide himself, far less another. But now, I think I can answer for him, or if I cannot, she can, for she appears to have most influence over him now——What do you say, then? Shall we let them have each other? There is no hurry, but neither do I see why we should wait. You, Guttorm, are a well-to-do man; I, certainly, am not quite so rich, and I have several to provide for; but at the same time I see no obstacle. Say now what you think of it——as for *her*, I'll ask her last, for I think I know her mind."

Thus Sämund. Guttorm sat, bent forward,

putting each hand by turns upon the other. He made repeated attempts at drawing himself up, but did not succeed without four or five deep-drawn breaths. Then only he got his back straight, and stroking his knee he sat looking at his wife in a way which included Synnövé in his gaze.

But the wife sat mute. No one could judge from the expression of her face. She sat at the table, her forefinger drawing figures upon it, as before.

"This is no doubt a very handsome offer," she said at last.

"It seems to me we might do worse than accept it with thanks," replied Guttorm, and looked as though he felt immensely relieved by this statement, his eye gliding from Karen to Sämund and back to Karen.

"We have but this one child," continued she; "we must consider."

"There is no reason why you should not," rejoined Sämund; "at the same time, I do not see what should hinder an immediate reply—as the bear said, having asked the peasant for his cow."

"Yes, I think we might give an answer," said Guttorm, still looking at his wife.

"We might—only that Thorbjörn is somewhat wild."

"As to that, I think I have observed him changed lately," replied Guttorm——"You know yourself what you said this very morning——"

Thereupon the husband and wife sat gazing at one another, a full minute, silently.

"If one could but be sure of him," said she at last.

"Well," interposed Sämund again, "as to that, I can but repeat what I have said already; it will be steady driving if she keeps a hold on the reins. It is marvellous what power she has over him. I saw that more and more when he lay ill, and we knew not what the end might be —whether he would rise again or not."

"You must not hold out any longer, wife— you know *her* mind, and after all *her* happiness is ours!"

At these words Synnöve for the first time raised her eyes, looking at her father with deep, glowing gratitude.

"Yes, yes," said Karen, her finger gliding faster and faster over the table; "if I have put myself against it till now, it was just because of that——and perhaps I did not feel as hard as I spoke——"

She looked up smiling, but tears stood in her eyes. And Guttorm rose.

"It has come about, then, what I have wished for more than anything else in life," said he, and walked across to Synnöve.

"I have never doubted but that it would come about," said Sămund, rising also; "if two are meant for one another, they'll get one another." And he joined the others.

"But what does the child say to it all?" asked the mother, who also had moved towards Synnöve.

. The girl kept her seat, motionless. They all surrounded her, except Thorbjörn, who was still sitting where he had first sat down.

"You must get up, my child," whispered the mother.

She rose, smiled, and turned her face away, for the tears were coming.

"The dear Lord be with thee, now and

always," continued the mother, taking her to her arms and crying with her.

The two men walked away, each in a different direction.

"You must go to him now," said the mother, loosing her hold and pushing her forward gently.

Synnövé walked a step and stood still ; it seemed impossible to proceed. But Thorbjörn started up, and, approaching her, seized her hand ; not knowing, however, whether he might do more, he stood before her holding it, until she withdrew it slowly.

And thus they stood, face to face, in silence.

At this moment the door was opened noiselessly, and a head appeared.

"Is Synnövé here ? " asked a shy little voice. It was Ingrid Granliden.

"Yes, she is ; come in," said her father. Ingrid hesitated.

"Come in ; it's settled now," added he.

They all looked at her. She seemed embarrassed.

"There is some one else outside," she said at last.

"Who is it ? " asked Guttorm.

"It's the mother," she answered, softly.

"Let her come in!" four voices exclaimed at once; and Karen walked to the door, the others looking well pleased.

"Come in, mother," they heard Ingrid say, "it is all well." And Ingeborg Granliden, in her snow-white cap, entered the room.

"I guessed that something was happening," she said, "although Sämund keeps his own counsel. And we two could not refrain from coming."

"Yes," returned Sämund, "just that has happened that you wished for most." And he stepped aside that she might approach the young people.

"May God bless you for having drawn him towards you," said Ingeborg, taking Synnöve to her heart, holding her fast. "You have kept faith to the last, my child; and see, your desire has been given you." She stroked the girl's cheeks gently. Her own tears fell fast, she heeded them not, but wiped Synnöve's carefully and tenderly.

"Yes, and it is after all a fine lad whom you now have——I need no longer fear for him." And again she pressed Synnövé to her heart.

"The mother understands her chickens better than we who supposed ourselves so wise," remarked Sämund.

Their happiness grew quiet at last. Karen began to think of supper, begging little Ingrid to assist her, "for Synnövé is no good to-night," she said; and the two were soon busy preparing the evening meal, while the men talked about the harvest.

Thorbjörn was sitting apart at the window, when Synnövé, approaching him softly, laid her hand on his shoulder.

"What are you looking at?" she whispered.

He turned his head, gazed long and tenderly into her eyes, and glancing away again.

"I am looking at Granliden," he said—— "it is strange that I can look at it now from Solbakken——"

Printed by BALLANTYNE, HANSON & Co.
London & Edinburgh

𝔄 Selection

FROM

MR. WM. HEINEMANN'S LIST

—————

REMBRANDT: His Life, His Work, and
His Time. By ÉMILE MICHEL. Translated by FLORENCE
SIMMONDS. Edited and prefaced by FREDERICK WEDMORE.
With 67 Plates and 250 Illustrations in the Text. 2 vols.,
royal 8vo, £2 2s. net. Also an Edition on Japanese paper,
limited to 150 Copies. Price on application.

A FRIEND OF THE QUEEN. MARIE
ANTOINETTE AND COUNT FERSEN. By PAUL
GAULOT. Translated from the French by Mrs. CASHEL
HOEY. In 2 vols., 8vo. With 2 Portraits. Price 24s.

THE ROMANCE OF AN EMPRESS.
CATHERINE II. OF RUSSIA. By R. WALISZEWSKI.
Translated from the French. Second Edition. 8vo. With
Portrait. Price 7s. 6d.

MEMOIRS. By CHARLES GODFREY LELAND
(HANS BREITMANN). Second Edition. 8vo. With Portrait. Price 7s. 6d.

VILLIERS DE L'ISLE ADAM: His Life
and Works. From the French of VICOMTE ROBERT DU
PONTAVICE DE HEUSSEY. By LADY MARY LOYD. With
Portrait and Facsimile. Crown 8vo, cloth, 10s. 6d.

ALFRED, LORD TENNYSON. A Study of
His Life and Work. By ARTHUR WAUGH, B.A. Oxon.
With 5 Portraits, and 20 Illustrations from Photographs
specially taken for this work. New Edition. Crown 8vo,
cloth, 7s. 6d.

TWENTY-FIVE YEARS IN THE SECRET
SERVICE. The Recollections of a Spy. By Major
LE CARON. In One Volume, 8vo. With Portraits and
Facsimiles. 14s. Also Popular Edition, crown 8vo, boards,
2s. 6d., cloth, 3s. 6d.

THE GREAT WAR OF 189-. A Forecast.

By Rear-Admiral COLOMB, Col. MAURICE, R.A., Major HENDERSON, Staff College, Captain MAUDE, ARCHIBALD FORBES, CHARLES LOWE, D. CHRISTIE MURRAY, F. SCUDAMORE, and Sir CHARLES DILKE. In 1 vol., 8vo, illustrated. 12s. 6d.

LOVE SONGS OF ENGLISH POETS,

1500-1800. With Notes by RALPH H. CAINE. Fcap. 8vo, cloth extra, 3s. 6d.
₊ Also 100 Copies printed on Hand-made paper, 10s. 6d. net.

GOSSIP IN A LIBRARY. By EDMUND GOSSE.

Second Edition. Crown 8vo, gilt top, 7s. 6d.
₊ Large Paper Edition, limited to 100 copies. Price 25s. net.

QUESTIONS AT ISSUE. Essays. By EDMUND

GOSSE. Crown 8vo, buckram, gilt top, 7s. 6d.
₊ A Limited Edition on Large Paper, 25s. net.

THE ROSE: A Treatise on the Cultivation,

History, Family Characteristics, &c., of the Various Groups of Roses. With Accurate Description of the Varieties now Generally Grown. By H. B. ELLWANGER. With an Introduction by GEORGE H. ELLWANGER. 12mo, cloth, 5s.

THE GARDEN'S STORY ; or, Pleasures and

Trials of an Amateur Gardener. By G. H. ELLWANGER. With an Introduction by the Rev. C. WOLLEY DOD. 12mo, cloth, with illustrations, 5s.

THE KINGDOM OF GOD IS WITHIN

YOU. Christianity not as a Mystic Religion but as a New Theory of Life. By COUNT LEO TOLSTOY. Translated from the Russian by CONSTANCE GARNETT. Library Edition, in 2 vols, crown 8vo, 10s. Also a Popular Edition in 1 vol., cloth, 2s. 6d.

THE OLD MAIDS' CLUB. By I. ZANGWILL,

Author of "The Bachelor's Club," &c. With Illustrations by F. H. TOWNSEND. Crown 8vo, 3s. 6d.

WOMAN—THROUGH A MAN'S EYE-

GLASS. By MALCOLM C. SALAMAN. With Illustrations by DUDLEY HARDY. Crown 8vo, 3s. 6d.

FROM WISDOM COURT. By H. S. MERRI-

MAN and S. G. TALLENTYRE. With 30 Illustrations by E. COURBOIN. Crown 8vo, 3s. 6d.

THE GENTLE ART OF MAKING ENE-

MIES. By J. M'NEILL WHISTLER. *A New Edition.* In One Volume, pott 4to, 10s. 6d.

THE WORKS OF HEINRICH HEINE.
Translated by CHARLES G. LELAND, F.R.L.S., M.A. The Prose Works in Eight Volumes. In cloth cabinet price £2 10s., or separately 5s. per volume. Volume I., Florentine Nights, Schnabelewopski, The Rabbi of Bacharach, and Shakespeare's Maidens and Women. Volumes II. and III., Pictures of Travel. In Two Volumes. Volume IV., The Salon. Volumes V. and VI., Germany. In Two Volumes. Volumes VII. and VIII., French Affairs. In Two Volumes.

THE FAMILY LIFE OF HEINRICH
HEINE. Illustrated by one hundred and twenty-two hitherto unpublished letters addressed by him to different members of his family. Edited by his nephew Baron LUDWIG VON EMBDEN, and translated by CHARLES GODFREY LELAND. In One Volume, 8vo, with 4 Portraits. 12s. 6d.

DE QUINCEY MEMORIALS. Edited by
ALEXANDER H. JAPP, LL.D., F.R.S.E. In Two Volumes. Demy 8vo, with Portrait, 30s. net.

THE POSTHUMOUS WORKS OF
THOMAS DE QUINCEY. Edited by ALEXANDER H. JAPP, LL.D., F.R.S.E. Volume I. Suspiria de Profundis and other Essays. Volume II. Conversation and Coleridge, and other Essays. Crown 8vo, 6s. each.

The Great Educators.

Each subject complete in one volume.
Crown 8vo, price 5s. each.

ARISTOTLE, and the Ancient Educational
Ideals. By THOMAS DAVIDSON, M.A., LL.D.

LOYOLA, and the Educational System of the
Jesuits. By Rev. THOMAS HUGHES, S.J.

ALCUIN, and the Rise of the Christian
Schools. By Professor ANDREW F. WEST, Ph.D.

FROEBEL, and Education by Self-Activity.
By H. COURTHOPE BOWEN, M.A.

ABELARD, and the Origin and Early History
of Universities. By JULES GABRIEL COMPAYRÉ, Professor in the Faculty of Toulouse.

Others in preparation.

New Six Shilling Volumes.

THE HEAVENLY TWINS. By SARAH GRAND,
Author of " Ideala," &c.

IDEALA. By SARAH GRAND.

OUR MANIFOLD NATURE. By SARAH
GRAND. With Portrait of the Author.

A SUPERFLUOUS WOMAN.

THE STORY OF A MODERN WOMAN.
By ELLA HEPWORTH DIXON.

THE LAST SENTENCE. By MAXWELL
GRAY, Author of " The Silence of Dean Maitland," &c.

APPASSIONATA: A Musician's Story. By
ELSA D'ESTERRE-KEELING.

FROM THE FIVE RIVERS. By FLORA
ANNIE STEEL, Author of " The Potter's Thumb."

RELICS. Fragments of a Life. By FRANCES
MACNAB.

THE TOWER OF TADDEO. By OUIDA.

THE O'CONNORS OF BALLINAHINCH.
By Mrs. HUNGERFORD, Author of " Molly Bawn."

THE KING OF SCHNORRERS, GRO-
TESQUES AND FANTASIES. By I. ZANGWILL.
With over Ninety Illustrations.

CHILDREN OF THE GHETTO. By I.
ZANGWILL.

THE PREMIER AND THE PAINTER.
A Fantastic Romance. By I. ZANGWILL and LOUIS COWEN.

THE RECIPE FOR DIAMONDS. By C. J.
CUTLIFFE HYNE.

THE COUNTESS RADNA. By W. E. NORRIS.

THE NAULAHKA. A Tale of West and
East. By RUDYARD KIPLING and WOLCOTT BALESTIER.

AVENGED ON SOCIETY. By H. F. WOOD,
Author of " The Englishman of the Rue Cain."

Heinemann's International Library.

Edited by EDMUND GOSSE. Price 3s. 6d. cloth, 2s. 6d. paper.

* Each Volume has an Introduction specially written
by the Editor.

New Review.—"If you have any pernicious remnants of literary chauvinism, I hope it will not survive the series of foreign classics of which Mr. William Heinemann, aided by Mr. Edmund Gosse, is publishing translations to the great contentment of all lovers of literature."

Times.—"A venture which deserves encouragement."

IN GOD'S WAY. From the Norwegian of BJÖRNSTJERNE BJÖRNSON.

PIERRE AND JEAN. From the French of GUY DE MAUPASSANT.

THE CHIEF JUSTICE. From the German of KARL EMIL FRANZOS, Author of "For the Right," &c.

WORK WHILE YE HAVE THE LIGHT. From the Russian of COUNT TOLSTOY.

FANTASY. From the Italian of MATILDE SERAO.

FROTH. From the Spanish of DON ARMANDO PALACIO VALDÉS.

FOOTSTEPS OF FATE. From the Dutch of LOUIS COUPERUS.

PEPITA JIMÉNEZ. From the Spanish of JUAN VALERA.

THE COMMODORE'S DAUGHTERS. From the Norwegian of JONAS LIE.

THE HERITAGE OF THE KURTS. From the Norwegian of BJÖRNSTJERNE BJÖRNSON.

LOU. From the German of BARON VON ROBERTS.

DOÑA LUZ. From the Spanish of JUAN VALERA.

THE JEW. From the Polish of JOSEPH IGNATIUS KRASZEWSKI.

UNDER THE YOKE. From the Bulgarian of IVAN VAZOFF.

FAREWELL LOVE! From the Italian of MATILDE SERAO.

THE GRANDEE. From the Spanish of Don ARMANDO PALACIO VALDÉS.

popular 3s. 6d. Novels.

ACCORDING TO ST. JOHN. By AMÉLIE RIVES, Author of "The Quick or the Dead."

ORIOLE'S DAUGHTER. By JESSIE FOTHER-GILL, Author of "The First Violin," &c.

THE MASTER OF THE MAGICIANS. By ELIZABETH STUART PHELPS and HERBERT D. WARD.

THE HEAD OF THE FIRM. By Mrs. RIDDELL, Author of "George Geith," "Maxwell Drewett," &c.

THE STORY OF A PENITENT SOUL. Being the Private Papers of Mr. Stephen Dart, late Minister at Lynnbridge, in the County of Lincoln. By ADELINE SERGEANT, Author of "No Saint," &c.

NOR WIFE, NOR MAID. By Mrs. HUNGERFORD, Author of "Molly Bawn," &c.

THE HOYDEN. By Mrs. HUNGERFORD.

MAMMON. A Novel. By Mrs. ALEXANDER, Author of "The Wooing O't," &c.

DAUGHTERS OF MEN. By HANNAH LYNCH, Author of "The Prince of the Glades," &c.

A LITTLE MINX. By ADA CAMBRIDGE, Author of "A Marked Man," &c.

A MARKED MAN : Some Episodes in his Life. By ADA CAMBRIDGE.

THE THREE MISS KINGS. By ADA CAMBRIDGE.

NOT ALL IN VAIN. By ADA CAMBRIDGE.

A KNIGHT OF THE WHITE FEATHER. By TASMA, Author of "The Penance of Portia James," "Uncle Piper of Piper's Hill," &c.

UNCLE PIPER OF PIPER'S HILL. By TASMA.

THE PENANCE OF PORTIA JAMES. By TASMA.

Popular 3s. 6d. Novels.

THE SCAPEGOAT. By HALL CAINE, Author
of " The Bondman," &c.

THE BONDMAN. A New Saga. By HALL
CAINE.

CAPT'N DAVY'S HONEYMOON, The
Blind Mother, and The Last Confession. By HALL
CAINE.

THE RETURN OF THE O'MAHONY.
By HAROLD FREDERIC, Author of " In the Valley," &c.
With Illustrations.

IN THE VALLEY. By HAROLD FREDERIC.
With Illustrations.

THE COPPERHEAD, and other Stories of the
North during the American War. By HAROLD FREDERIC.

KITTY'S FATHER. By FRANK BARRETT,
Author of " The Admirable Lady Biddy Fane," &c.

MR. BAILEY-MARTIN. By PERCY WHITE.

A QUESTION OF TASTE. By MAARTEN
MAARTENS, Author of "'An Old Maid's Love," &c.

COME LIVE WITH ME AND BE MY
LOVE. By ROBERT BUCHANAN, Author of "The
Moment After," " The Coming Terror," &c.

A ROMANCE OF THE CAPE FRONTIER.
By BERTRAM MITFORD, Author of " Through the Zulu
Country," &c.

'TWEEN SNOW AND FIRE. A Tale of the
Kafir War of 1877. By BERTRAM MITFORD.

Popular Shilling Books.

PRETTY MISS SMITH. By FLORENCE
WARDEN, Author of the " The House on the Marsh," &c.

MADAME VALERIE. By F. C. PHILIPS,
Author of " As in a Looking-Glass," &c.

THE MOMENT AFTER. A Tale of the Un-
seen. By ROBERT BUCHANAN.

CLUES; or, Leaves from a Chief Constable's
Note-Book. By WILLIAM HENDERSON, Chief Constable
of Edinburgh.

Dramatic Literature.

THE PLAYS OF ARTHUR W. PINERO.

Price 1s. 6d. each paper cover, 2s. 6d. cloth.

I. The Times.   II. The Profligate.   III. The Cabinet Minister.   IV. The Hobby-Horse.   V. Lady Bountiful.   VI. The Magistrate.   VII. Dandy Dick.   VIII. Sweet Lavender.   IX. The Schoolmistress.

THE MASTER BUILDER.

A Play in four Acts. By HENRIK IBSEN. Translated by EDMUND GOSSE and W. ARCHER. Small 4to, with Portrait, 5s. Popular Edition, paper, 1s.

BRAND.

A Dramatic Poem in Five Acts. By HENRIK IBSEN. Translated in the original metre with an Introduction and Notes by C. H. HERFORD. Small 4to. 7s. 6d.

HEDDA GABLER.

A Drama in Four Acts. By HENRIK IBSEN. Translated by EDMUND GOSSE. Small 4to, with Portrait, 5s. Vaudeville Edition, paper, 1s.

⁎ A limited Large Paper Edition, with three Portraits, 21s. net.

THE FRUITS OF ENLIGHTENMENT.

A Comedy in Four Acts. By LYOF TOLSTOY. Translated from the Russian by E. J. DILLON. With an Introduction by A. W. PINERO, and a Portrait of the Author. Small 4to, 5s.

THE PRINCESS MALEINE.

Translated from the French by GERARD HARRY; and THE INTRUDER. By MAURICE MAETERLINCK. Translated from the French. With an Introduction by HALL CAINE. Small 4to, with a Portrait. 5s.

THE LIFE OF HENRIK IBSEN.

By HENRIK JÆGER. Translated by CLARA BELL. With the Verse done into English from the Norwegian original by EDMUND GOSSE. In One Volume, crown 8vo, 6s.

A COMMENTARY ON THE WORKS OF HENRIK IBSEN.

By HJALMAR HJORTH BOYESEN, Author of "Goethe and Schiller," "Essays on German Literature," &c. Crown 8vo, cloth, 7s. 6d. net.